LOVE POTION:
A MEDICAL THRILLER

THE CIA WANTS THE DRUG AND WILL KILL TO GET IT...

Enjoy! Remember it's only fiction

Allan Zelinger

ISBN: 1500150363
ISBN 13: 9781500150365
Library of Congress Control Number: 2014910792
CreateSpace Independent Publishing Platform
North Charleston, South Carolina

1

The accused sat with his attorney in a small conference room at the courthouse. An armed guard was stationed just outside the door. Aaron Sharpton slowly picked at the cold lunch he was served while wearing handcuffs. Meanwhile, the lawyer thumbed through a newspaper, grunting when he read something of interest. Both expected to spend their afternoon together while the jury deliberated.

Once court adjourned, Sharpton, who had been denied bail, would be remanded back to his prison cell while the sequestered jury headed off to its secret hotel accommodations. The process could drag on for days. When it was over, Sharpton and his attorney hoped it would end with a hung jury or by some miracle, a not-guilty judgment.

Suddenly the guard stuck his head in and told them, "Court reconvenes in fifteen minutes."

The two looked at each other, dumbfounded by the speed at which a decision had been reached. "Ah, shit!" Sharpton exclaimed. "That ain't no good." A verdict reached after only three hours, could only mean one thing…guilt.

The empty courtroom filled quickly with those eager to hear the result after ten days of emotionally grueling testimony. Everyone stood as Judge Hazelton, black robes flowing, entered and took his seat. He was glad the arduous trial would soon be over.

"Have the members of the jury reached their decision?" The judge asked.

"Yes, we have, Your Honor," the foreman answered. He handed a folded piece of paper to the bailiff, who passed it to the judge. Hazelton put on bifocals, and looked at what was written.

"Will the defendant rise and face the jury," Hazelton ordered. Next he instructed the foreman, "Please announce the verdict to the court?"

"On count one, the death of Marshall Dixon, we find the defendant guilty of murder in the second degree." The foreman continued. "On count two, the death of Shakira Williams, we find the defendant guilty of murder in the second degree. On count three, the death of an unborn child, we find the defendant guilty of murder in the second degree."

No sooner did he finish his last pronouncement than a woman who was sitting in the courtroom jumped up from her seat and began screaming at Sharpton, "I hope you burn in hell, you goddamn animal!" Restrained by family members and friends, Shakira's despondent mother was helped back down into her seat.

At the verdict's reading, Sharpton showed no emotion. The handsome African-American man with piercing blue eyes stood before the court wearing a fine tailored suit and tie. Except for his handcuffs and leg shackles, he looked more like a model from an issue of *GQ* than a man just convicted of multiple murders.

Judge Hazelton spoke. "Before we leave, let me take a moment to make a personal statement." He paused, took off his bifocals and glared down at Sharpton. "In all my years serving on the bench, I have never seen such a wanton act of savage violence as the one, which you, Mr. Sharpton, have been found guilty of committing. This Commonwealth will be a safer place with you put away behind bars. Exactly how long civil society will be spared your presence shall be determined tomorrow."

Hazelton slammed his gavel down hard then pronounced, "We stand adjourned until ten a.m. for sentencing."

Sharpton knew there was no death penalty in Massachusetts, so he wasn't going to burn in hell anytime soon, as Shakira's mother had implored. He would just be sent away for the next thirty-five to fifty years, depending on tomorrow's hearing. As far as what the judge said to him, the man was entirely correct. He had committed a despicable crime, and deserved to be punished. Sharpton only wished to God he could somehow have averted the fit of blind rage that had possessed him which led to the deaths of Dixon and Shakira. Even more regretful, his actions had unwittingly taken the life of his own unborn son.

Sharpton's five-hundred-dollar-an-hour lawyer, one of the top criminal defense attorneys in Boston, patted his client on the back in consolation. "Don't worry. I'll have your appeal filed before the sentencing hearing gets started."

Guards led the prisoner out of the courtroom, shuffling in leg-irons. Aaron realized he was not going to be a free man for a very long time, but in prison, might actually end up living longer. His life up until now had not been conducive to longevity.

Heading down the court hallway to a van that would transport him to jail, Aaron recalled being shot in a rival gang's assassination attempt and lay on the street pavement. He was bleeding from bullet holes in his chest and abdomen. Looking up, he saw the face of a paramedic and heard him say, "This gangbanger is a goner," just before losing consciousness.

Days later he awoke in a hospital bed, tubes coming out of every orifice. When the one in his throat was finally removed and Aaron could speak, he asked his nurse in a raspy voice, "What the hell happened to me?"

"You lost so much blood by the time you hit our emergency room your heart stopped. They gave you CPR all the way to the operating room," she answered.

"Do you mean I was dead?"

"Well, it took thirty minutes of pumping on your chest until they brought you back."

"Damn, I don't remember seeing no white light or nothin'. I guess all that afterlife shit is just a big scam like everything else." Aaron laughed, then winced with pain. "Shit, my chest hurts like hell."

"Hang on. I'll get you some pain medicine."

The nurse left the room, then quickly returned with a syringe containing morphine. She injected the medication intravenously, and his pain quickly subsided.

"That's pretty good stuff," he said, slurring his words as the narcotic took affect. "I'll take another hit if you don't mind."

"Not for the next four hours, you won't. It's the doctor's order."

"He isn't the one who's hurting."

A few weeks later, Aaron was discharged from the hospital, lucky to be alive but ready to resume his leadership of the Boston's most notorious gang, the Vice Lords.

2

Dr. Gabriel Schaeffer was standing in front of the elevator bank on the fifth floor at Boston General. He had just finished making rounds on the psych ward and was going over to the ambulatory care building for his afternoon clinic. Gabe turned his head toward the television in the visitors waiting area when he heard the newsman say something that caught his attention.

Verdict was reached today in a trial that has captivated our city's interest over the last two weeks. The reputed head of Boston's most notorious street gang, Aaron Sharpton, was found guilty in the brutal slayings of his girlfriend, Shakira Williams, and Marshall Dixon, a fellow gang member. Because Ms. Williams was pregnant at the time of the murder, Sharpton was also convicted in the death of her unborn child.

The jury deliberation ended swiftly, and sentencing is expected tomorrow. Sharpton faces a minimum of thirty-five years behind bars. Leaving the courthouse, Mr. Sharpton's well-known criminal attorney, Randy Specter, promised to immediately file for appeal.

The elevator door suddenly opened, and Gabe stepped in trying not to spill the cup of coffee in his hand. He had a special interest in Sharpton's case. As court-appointed expert, Gabe performed an extensive psychiatric evaluation on the accused. He had spent hours with the defendant, locked inside a dingy room at the prison, taking Sharpton's life history, then administering the psychometric testing necessary to reach a conclusion regarding his ability to stand trial.

Inside the elevator Gabe shook his head in dismay, realizing Sharpton would now end up spending most of his life behind bars. True, Sharpton was found guilty of committing heinous crimes, but Gabe was convinced that with proper treatment, he could have prevented them from happening in the first place.

Schaeffer was a recognized authority on violent behavior. His expert testimony was often sought in cases where the sheer brutality of a crime raised questions about the sanity of its perpetrator.

He learned a lot about Sharpton during their pretrial sessions. When they first met, the prisoner was brought into the interview room in handcuffs and leg shackles.

"Could you please take those off?" Gabe asked the guard.

"But Doc, this guy has been accused of three murders."

"I can't do my evaluation on a man in chains. Please undo them."

"Well…okay if you insist," the guard reluctantly agreed. "I'll be right outside just in case."

Once they were alone, Gabe pulled out a file and pen from inside his briefcase, then began the conversation.

"Aaron, I'm Gabriel Schaeffer, the court-appointed doctor assigned to your case."

"Oh, you're the one who's supposed to find out whether I'm a psycho."

"Well, I might not say it that way, but I do have to determine your mental fitness to stand trial. Hope you don't mind if I ask you some personal questions?"

"Sure, fire away. I've got nothing better on my schedule today than looking at the walls of my cell. Go right ahead and ask whatever you want."

"Why don't we start by you telling me a little about your childhood?"

"What's to tell? I'm just another poor black kid from Roxbury with a *crackhead* for a mother, and no father around. I was on the streets fending for myself from day one."

"You went to church, didn't you?"

"How'd you know about that?"

"I reviewed the investigator's file."

"Yeah, I went there, but not to pray. Reverend Sykes, our neighborhood preacher, took a liking to me and used to lend me books. I spent time in church because it was the only quiet place around to read."

"Did you like going to school?"

"Well, at least I got a real meal there now and then." Aaron paused briefly before continuing. "I imagine if you saw my records, you probably know I messed up one of my teachers pretty bad."

"Tell me about that."

"Well, I was bored to tears in his math class, and he knew it. I'd get a perfect score on every exam, but the guy just didn't like me. Every once in a while I'd correct an equation he put on the blackboard. Maybe that pissed him off. So he gives me a C instead of the A that I deserved, but no big deal. I'm not going to sweat it over some dumb ass teacher with a bad attitude.

"Then one day I was talking to a friend at the back of his class. He walked up to me and says, 'Sharpton, you're nothing but ghetto scum.' The next thing I know, I whacked him pretty hard on the side of his head with my textbook. He ended up in the hospital for a few days, and I was suspended for a month."

"How did you feel about that?"

"Well, I didn't really mean to hurt him. I just saw red and reacted."

"Would you say that you have a short fuse?"

"I can get hot pretty quick, if that's what you mean." Aaron paused. "Say, if you're heading toward asking about what happened with Shakira and Dixon, my lawyer told me not to talk about it."

"No, you're absolutely correct, that's between you, your lawyer, and the authorities. I'm just looking for some background information. What about drugs? Do you think they have anything to do with your temper?"

"Doc, in my world everybody gets high once in a while, but you can't run an operation like I do all fucked-up on drugs or alcohol. The newspapers call it a *gang*, but it's really just a corporate enterprise with its own set of inner city rules. In my business I don't worry about IRS audits, I worry that the people who work for me could get shot and killed or end up getting arrested if I make a wrong move. Sure, I buy and distribute drugs, but don't use them myself."

***

The report Gabe submitted to the court concluded Aaron was perfectly sane and intellectually able to stand trial. However, one aspect of his assessment still gnawed at him. During his evaluation he found Aaron to have an exceptionally high IQ of 146. Aaron Sharpton, the accused murderer, also happened to be a genius. In Gabriel Schaeffer's mind, Aaron had more than enough smarts to have become the CEO of a Fortune 500 company, instead of ending up heading Boston's most notorious criminal gang. It was unfortunate circumstances of the blighted neighborhood he grew up in, coupled with a disturbed brain metabolism and lack of proper intervention that had determined Aaron's fate.

Gabe wouldn't soon forget his day spent in the courtroom waiting to testify at Sharpton's trial. Dr. Phillip Rhodes, a court-appointed forensic pathologist, was called to the stand first.

Before his testimony began, the judge requested that the courtroom be cleared of visitors, then cautioned the jury, "You are about to see photos taken at the crime scene. Some of you may be disturbed by the images."

Lights were dimmed, and the first photo came up on the screen. It showed a man lying in a pool of blood, his head turned at an impossible angle, his neck severed to the spine. Next, the photo of a female lying on her back came on. She had her throat slit as well and her eyes were still open staring blankly upward.

"The cause of death to the female was a single slicing knife wound to the neck," Rhodes said. "Her left carotid artery and internal jugular vein were severed, and she bled to death within minutes. At the time she expired my autopsy disclosed that Ms. Williams was four months pregnant."

Viewing the gruesome pictures of the murder scene, one juror vomited at her seat. Another fainted and had to be revived by smelling salts. The judge was forced to temporarily halt the proceedings.

On reconvening, Rhodes continued with his testimony. The prosecuting state's attorney, Blair Fiore, asked the pathologist, "Can you tell the court what the DNA analysis on the deceased disclosed?"

"We found no traces of Mr. Dixon's DNA on or in her person."

"By in, do you mean vaginal samples?"

"Yes, that is correct. Our methodology looks for sperm and Y chromosome DNA traces in vaginal samples. Although sperm may degrade from the sample after a number of days, the Y chromosome analysis remains positive for weeks after intercourse."

"Did you find any identifiable male DNA in those samples?"

"We found both sperm remnants and Y chromosome DNA belonging only to one individual."

"And who might that person be?"

"Mr. Sharpton."

"What about the DNA analysis on the fetus?" Fiore asked.

"The profile on the fetus unequivocally indicates that the genetic father was Mr. Aaron Sharpton."

The defendant suddenly jumped to his feet, pointed at Rhodes, and yelled, "You're a motherfucking liar! That kid was Dixon's, and Shakira cheated on me!"

Suddenly, Sharpton climbed onto the table in front of him, then jumped down and ran up to the witness box. He grabbed the startled pathologist by the throat. The man's eyes bulged as Aaron's strong hands tightened around his neck. Guards rushed up and tried to pull Sharpton away, but couldn't get him off. One of them pulled out a Taser and fired. Aaron fell onto the floor, contorting in spasms while Rhodes fought to catch his breath. Once Sharpton's arms and legs were secured, the guards dragged him out.

The trial resumed the next day. This time Sharpton was in handcuffs and leg-irons. Things were considerably less dramatic as Gabe gave his testimony confirming the defendant's sanity and intellectual ability to stand trial.

***

Sharpton's personality profile was not unusual for the violent persons Gabe studied. Most suffered from poor impulse control and little capacity to deal with frustration. The smallest provocation could at times set off a violent outburst endangering the lives of anyone around, including loved ones. Their formal diagnosis was IED, intermittent explosive disorder, which Gabe believed was caused not by bad upbringing but by disturbed neurochemistry deep inside the brain. Autopsy studies had never identified any consistent structural brain abnormality in such violence prone individuals. However, in Gabe's research he used a new and powerful functional MRI scanner to examine the intricate workings of the living brain.

The high technology scanner had disclosed something Gabe thought very important. There was abnormally high metabolic activity in a small area of the brain located within the amygdala, a region which controlled emotion and aggressive behavior.

With cooperation of the warden at Springhill's maximum-security prison, Gabe was able to study inmates with a history of violent crime using the MRI at Boston General Hospital. Those who signed Gabe's human experimentation permits were transported under guard to the General for their scans. The iron handcuffs they wore had to be switched to plastic before being brought near the strong magnetic field of the MRI for their test.

After Gabe processed the data, he found a similar abnormality in each, a tiny defective region smack-dab in the center of the amygdala. Once the results were published in the *Journal of Neurobehavioral Science*, they made headlines. Andrea Phelps, a reporter from CNN, interviewed Gabe on his research.

"Dr. Schaeffer, I understand you have found an abnormality in the brains of violent criminals that explains their behavior." A camera crew filmed as she spoke. "Does your work mean that extreme violence could be prevented?"

"Yes, my associate, Dr. Angela Chen, and I are working hard to understand the root cause of explosive violent behavior and hope it will lead to a treatment that could help prevent crime before it occurs."

"How would that be possible?"

"We are currently testing a drug which improves the disordered metabolism in a region of the brain where impulsive aggression has its origin. When we rescan our subjects who are taking the medication, their abnormality normalizes, and violent tendencies disappear."

"Do you mean that someday a pill will take the place of anger management classes and help prevent the violence so rampant in society today?"

"I'm sure there will always be a place for anger management counseling in milder cases but for those prone to severe violent outbursts, our medication may provide an answer. At least that's what our clinical experience suggests."

The cameraman turned to focus on the correspondent, who gave her concluding remarks. "It may be wishful thinking right now, but researchers like Drs. Schaeffer and Chen are using medical science to address one of the most serious problems plaguing our society today. What they propose isn't longer jail sentences, but rather preventing violent crime with the help of a special pill. I and everyone else watching should hope their solution works. This is Andrea Phelps for CNN, reporting from Boston General Hospital."

***

Aaron Sharpton was like so many of the others Gabe had evaluated: the middle-aged man who repeatedly stabbed his elderly father twenty four times because he wouldn't lend him money for a failing business, the policeman who shot his partner after he didn't stop for donuts and told him he was fat, the wife who used their son's baseball bat to beat her husband to death after she found out he had an affair. When Gabe studied their brain metabolism by MRI, all had the same abnormality, a pinpoint zone of derangement within their amygdala. The deficiency of modulating chemicals in that region of the brain leading to hyper-metabolic activity was like a loaded gun with a hairpin trigger—a slight provocation and sudden uncontrollable rage could result, destroying lives in the process.

***

After clinic Gabe stopped back at his office in the hospital. He was tired after a long day of work but sat down to type notes for the computerized charts of his outpatients seen earlier. When he was through, Gabe pulled Sharpton's folder from a file cabinet.

If his clinical research panned out with OX312, an amazing derivative of the hormone oxytocin, doctors would finally have something to offer people like Aaron Sharpton. A treatment that would stop the tendency to episodic violence could make a huge difference in the lives of so many.

Sharpton's trial was over a year ago, and he was now an inmate at Springhill Penitentiary. For the last six months, Sharpton had been enrolled as a subject in Gabe's research, taking a daily dose of OX312, and his response was nothing short of miraculous. Aaron was a model prisoner who was now taking college classes over the Internet. If his ambitions came to fruition, and in Gabe's opinion they would, the man who had committed brutal murders, a feared leader of Boston's Vice Lords gang, would one day be the first prisoner to ever graduate both college and law school from behind bars at Springhill.

3

Scott Ferguson sat behind the desk in his office at the Defense Department. His feet were propped up on a windowsill, and he was looking outside. Ferguson relished his view of DC with the Capitol dome in the distance almost as much as the power his post gave him. A career soldier with the rank of colonel, Ferguson had chiseled features, and his thick pepper-gray hair sported a crew cut. At forty-four he figured he wasn't doing badly and might even be up for advancement to brigadier general by next year.

Although out of active combat duty for some time, he did a daily exercise routine of push-ups, sit-ups, and jumping jacks to maintain combat-ready fitness. Wearing his army uniform, Ferguson looked every bit the quintessential soldier.

At his current post in the Defense, Ferguson was in charge of disbursing funds for the myriad of medical research projects supported by the military. Each year millions of dollars were spent by the Defense Department on medical research. The studies spanned an enormous gamut, everything from using stem cells to reduce tissue damage produced by shrapnel to examining the effect of sleep disorders on performance. Research on anything that could potentially impair or improve the ability of the American soldier in battle was fair game to receive financial support from the office Ferguson commanded.

A knock on his door broke the colonel's reverie. He pulled his legs off the windowsill, turned around in his chair, and sat erect, clearing his throat before he spoke.

"Come on in," Ferguson barked. Lieutenant Russell Holmes, his military attaché, entered. "You said you had something for me?" Ferguson asked.

"Yes sir, I thought you might find this interesting."

"What is it?"

"A study we have funded using an experimental drug called OX312. The purported effect was modulation of aggression by altering brain neurochemistry. The principal investigator is Dr. Gabriel Schaeffer, a staff psychiatrist at Boston General Hospital, and his co-investigator Angela Chen, a PhD in neurobiology, also at Boston General."

"Russell, so far I'm bored as hell."

"Don't be, sir, please listen," he politely requested of his superior.

Ferguson sat back in his chair and prepared to hear Holmes out.

"They originally used OX312 to study its effect on aggressive behavior in laboratory animals, and Defense financed their five-year grant. We supported their work thinking that the drug might one day be of use to us by improving our troops' combat performance."

"And how might that be?"

"Sir, by helping our men to be more fiercely aggressive warriors on the battlefield," Holmes answered.

"Jesus, Holmes, you're putting me to sleep." Ferguson said as he stretched his arms and yawned.

"The human clinical study Dr. Schaeffer initiated involves a group of hardened criminals. Each had a record of highly aggressive behavior in his past, and at least one felony conviction for a serious violent crime leading to the incarceration."

"Well, I said I'd listen, but—"

"Please, sir." Holmes glanced down at the file of papers he held and went on. "After a few days of treatment with OX312, violent behavior that characterized the inmates abated."

"So, who gives a shit?"

"Well, sir, hear me out. The correctional officers report being shocked by the dramatic changes in inmate behavior. Incorrigibly violent prisoners no longer required restraints. They were able to live among other inmates rather than remain in constant isolation. Hell, they report skinheads eating together in the mess hall with blacks and Hispanics. On OX312 it appears any tendency for violent behavior simply disappeared.

"Their five-year grant was up for midterm review, and they were required to submit a report to our office. That's when I found this out."

"OK, so what of it?"

Russell thought for a moment before going on. "Well, we funded the research thinking it might result in a drug that would improve troop performance, not turn them into wussies. Imagine if some enemy power managed to get hold of this and use it into our men? That could very well endanger our national security."

"Don't be ridiculous. Who would do anything like that?"

"Sir, it's not farfetched at all," Holmes said. "Let me remind you that during the Cold War, we got wind that the Russians bought a truckload of lysergic dimethyl acid, commonly known as LSD, from a Swiss pharmaceutical company, and were planning to use it for military purposes. Defense went so far as to begin studying the effects of LSD on our own troops, wondering if there was a way to aerosolize it for use back on the Ruskies. Hell, if a soldier is hallucinating pink elephants he can't be very effective in battle."

"I suppose you're right on that."

"Yes, and that's not all. It's well documented our CIA used LSD in project MKULTRA, during the nineteen sixties, trying to achieve mind control and get communist spies to tell all during difficult interrogations. However, they found the effects of LSD were too erratic to be deployed for that purpose. So, sir, I would have to say that a drug like OX312 could prove quite dangerous if it got in the wrong hands."

"Holmes, how'd you know about all that shit?"

"It's my job to know that kind of shit, sir."

"Then kill the goddamned project. Pull the plug on our funding and insist that we retain rights to the OX...whatever it was."

"It was OX312, sir, and I'm not sure I can do that."

"Well, why not?"

"The compound didn't originate at Defense. Schaeffer and his colleague, Angela Chen, hold rights to the agent.

"Then buy it from them. We're the US government. They can't refuse."

"I'll try, sir."

"What do you mean, try? You'll get it done and that's an order."

"Yes sir."

"And keep me informed, you hear?"

"I will, sir."

Holmes saluted, did an about-face, and marched out the door. Ferguson took a cigar out of the humidor on his desk and lit it. He inhaled the rich tobacco smoke deeply, then blew a ring up toward the ceiling. Ferguson swiveled around in his chair, put his feet up on the window sill, and once again looked out at the Capitol building in the distance.

4

Angela Chen sat in her office at the Boston General Research Building reviewing a paper she was about to submit. After receiving her PhDs in both psychology and neurobiology from Harvard, Angela applied for the coveted position of research associate in the Department of Psychiatry at Boston General and was chosen.

Her work involved collaborating with Gabriel Schaeffer, one of the foremost psychiatrists in the country, and a person she greatly admired. It was over two years ago, but Angela still recalled the phone call when she told Gabe about her findings using OX312.

"Can I speak with Dr. Schaeffer?" Angela had asked the secretary at the outpatient psych clinic. She hated to interrupt him in the middle of his office hours but had to share the incredible news.

"I believe he's in with a patient right now," the secretary had said. "Can I leave Dr. Schaeffer a message?"

"No, I need to speak with him right away. Please tell him Angela is calling from our lab about something very important."

A minute later Gabe had come on the phone. "Angela, is something wrong?" He sounded worried. She had never before called during his office hours.

"Gabe, I'm really sorry to disturb you while you're with patients, but there's something I have to tell you right away."

Gabe had let out a sigh of relief. "Sure, go ahead, Angela, what is it?"

"Something unexpected is happening with the rats I gave the OX312."

"What do you mean? Is there some serious side effect?"

"No, it's nothing like that. Let me explain. OX312 is our modified derivative of the peptide, oxytocin. You know as well as I do that some call oxytocin the "love hormone," because it promotes sexual behavior in animals. However, my computer modeling indicated the modified version, OX312, was supposed to bind and activate a brain receptor in the amygdala that facilitates aggression. Instead, there was strong affinity for another receptor, one that happens to makes a world of difference in rat behavior."

"OK, fill me in quick because I have to get back to my patient."

"Well, I wouldn't exactly call it a 'side effect,' but the rats are behaving like they are falling in love with each other."

Gabe hadn't been able to keep himself from laughing. "Angela, this is no time for joking. I was in the middle of a treatment session."

"But, Gabe, this is no joke. The data is very clear."

"So go on and tell me about it."

"Every female rat given OX312 is posturing for sex as if she is in heat. But there's another odd thing. The male rats typically take multiple female partners, but the ones that got OX312 are acting strictly monogamous. They find one female, have sex, and then remain devoted to her. That same female will not posture any other male. I've never seen anything like this."

"You're telling me rats can fall in love?"

Angela had chuckled. "Not being of that species, I can't say for sure, but in terms of their behavior, that is how love might appear. I've not seen bonding like this before."

"Angela, I'm sorry to cut you short, but I've got to get back to my patient." He had paused and then went on. "However, what you're telling me sounds intriguing. We really need to sit down and go over the data together in detail. How about we meet for dinner tomorrow?"

"Sure, that would be fine. Just tell me where."

"Let's say about six thirty at the Shamrock?"

"See you there," Angela had told him.

As Gabe got off the phone with Angela, he had shaken his head and thought, *A drug that makes rats fall in love with each other, now that's a hoot.* But he had an office full of patients waiting to see him. Gabe had put on a serious face and reentered the examination room to complete his patient's treatment session. Further thought about OX312 with its unusual effect on his research assistant's experimental rats would have to wait.

***

Gabe had met Angela at the Shamrock for dinner the following evening. She had been waiting for him when Angela saw him enter through the door. Although he was her senior by a decade, she harbored a secret longing for him and wished he felt the same way about her. Unfortunately, he gave her no indication of interest in other than their research.

"Gabe, over here," Angela had called out, excitedly waving at him from the table. He couldn't hear his name over the loud noise, but then he saw her, and made his way over through the packed room.

"Boy, it's busy in here tonight," Gabe had said as he took a seat across from Angela.

"Yes, it's more crowded than usual, probably because there's a good band playing."

Gabe had settled into his chair, then with a smile said, "OK, now you can tell me a little more about rat love."

"Come on, Gabe. It's you that needs to be serious now. I've gone over the data very carefully. Here, see for yourself." Angela had pulled out a spreadsheet and handed it to her colleague. Gabe looked over the data. It corroborated what she told him. The rats treated with OX312 were forming lasting social bonds.

"Angela, I would have to agree. It appears you've discovered OX312 works like a love potion in rats. I thought it was supposed to make them nasty and more aggressive."

"It was, but biological systems are complex, and sometimes computer models don't predict what actually happens. Well, what I want to do next is design a clinical study using OX312 in persons having serious marital difficulties."

"But, Angela, love is a complex emotion. You can't manufacture it in pill form."

"Think about the thousands of couples having problems in their marriage. The divorce rate is fifty percent and climbing. Marital therapy costs a fortune and is often ineffective. What if taking OX312 helped couples stay together? If husbands and wives at each other's throats would fall back in love with a little pharmacologic assistance, it could make a huge difference. Think of all the families that could be saved from disruption by divorce. The entire fabric of our society could benefit."

"So you want to use this rodent *love* potion in humans, helping warring couples regain marital bliss."

"Sure, why not?"

"OK. But there's a big difference between rats and us. It might not work in humans."

Angela had given him a funny look, then said, "While we might look very different from lab rats, the chemical activity driving bonding relationships deep inside our brains may not be."

"Enough discussion, go ahead and draft a proposal for a study, and I will do what I can to get it approved by the research committee."

At the same time Gabe had agreed on helping Angela evaluate OX312 to achieve marital harmony, he had been thinking about something else. *What if I gave the drug to patients suffering with IED? I'm already counseling the inmates at Springhill. A study using OX312 shouldn't be hard to get through the General's human studies committee.*

Angela had stood up from her chair, walked around the table, and had given Gabe a kiss on his cheek.

"I can't thank you enough," she told Gabe as he blushed.

"Heck, it's the least I can do for you, Angela. You've put a tremendous amount of work into this project, and gotten some pretty interesting results."

They had spent the next hour discussing a possible scenario for her study protocol. "I'll have the details written up and on your desk for signature by the end of the week," she had told him. Then they parted, leaving the Shamrock, each going their separate ways.

5

G abe was driving to the maximum-security prison at Springhill. It had been nearly a year since he began the study on control of violent behavior in humans with IED using OX312. While the prisoners understood there was no quid pro quo to getting out earlier by participating, most took part in the medical research project because they wanted to do something that could benefit society. For many it represented their first time doing anything that approached being a noble, socially acceptable goal. All were felons convicted of at least one and sometimes multiple violent crimes.

Before Gabe enrolled anyone in his study, he and the inmate went over an extensive human study permission sheet that had been approved by the research committee at Boston General. While subjects received a nominal cash payment for their service, it was hardly enough to be considered a financial incentive. What the meager payment did allow for was purchase of an extra weekly snack from the prison commissary.

Dr. Schaeffer examined the study participants in a room adjacent to the prison infirmary. An armed guard was stationed nearby. After he arrived that morning, he met with Jerome Parker, an inmate serving an eight-year term for aggravated battery. He had used a rolling pin to beat the owner of a pizza parlor where he worked after his boss told him he didn't make his piecrust thin enough.

Gabe took the subject's blood pressure and heart rate, then asked, "So, Jerry, how are things going?"

"Well, I only have fifteen hundred and forty-three days left until I'm up for parole."

"What about the medication we started? How are you feeling?"

"Oh yeah, that pill. You know something, I do feel different."

"Can you tell me how?"

"It's hard to pinpoint, but I don't get upset like before. I used to go ballistic all the time. The asshole guards would get me ticked off about everything, and then end up dragging me into an isolation cell for a week."

"Get in any fights since our last meeting?"

"Nope. In fact, I'm offering my services free of charge to any inmate who wants them."

"What service is that?"

"Well, I'm a pretty good ink man. They call me *van Gogh* in here. I'm planning on opening my own tattoo shop as soon as I get out."

"That's great, Jerry. I'm really glad to hear you're doing so well, and making plans for the future. Let's see you again in four weeks for your next checkup."

"Thanks, Doc," the prisoner said, getting up and extending his hand to shake Gabe's. As Jerry was exiting he suddenly turned back and said, "Say, Doc Schaeffer, one more thing. Once I'm out of here, and get set up in my shop, if you happen to want a masterful piece of body art, the first tat is on the house!"

After Parker left, Gabe filled out a score of data sheets, grading his impression of the patient's behavior. Then he put the subject's file into his briefcase and prepared for the next evaluation.

It was late afternoon when he finished his last subject evaluation. The gate to the prison exit opened, and Gabe walked out, briefcase in hand. He left Springhill, driving back to Boston with evidence that OX312 was having a surprisingly beneficial effect on those taking it.

6

Paul Holfield was visiting Las Vegas. He was there negotiating with several relatively small pharma companies with an eye toward making an acquisition for the giant firm he now worked at, Novara. The main requirement for purchase was that the company had a signature drug that could potentially bolster Novara's pipeline.

Holfield presently occupied a position that was second-in-command to Gustav Jung, the CEO. Of late, with Jung acting like he was semi-retired, and spending much of his time traveling the world at leisure, Holfield was left in charge of day to day operations. According to the itinerary Jung had provided, the Novara CEO was on his yacht sailing around Bali.

Since joining up with the vaunted Swiss drug company, Holfield had adopted a serious work persona, one to match the rather stodgy professional demeanor of his boss. But since he wasn't in Switzerland, and Jung was on the other side of the globe, Holfield had every intention of having as much uninhibited fun in Vegas as he had in the past.

A creature of habit in many respects, Holfield felt quite at home in his penthouse suite at the Bellagio. Occupying a familiar lair atop the Las Vegas strip gave him a comforting feeling. The unique aspect of this visit was being accompanied on his trip there by a female, his administrative assistant and mistress, Inger Kroll.

***

He had to admit that Inger was amazing. She had an incredible body, could have sex tirelessly, and was independent enough that she didn't constantly cling to him. Holfield met her at a most unusual place—Grindelwald, Switzerland—while attending the funeral of his old boss, Rolfe Witig. By the time of Witig's death, Holfield had amicably left Celestica Pharmaceutical and taken up with Novara.

No one at the funeral knew that it was he who had torpedoed Witig and his company by sharing confidential data with rival Gustav Jung regarding complications associated with its newest product, Juvena.

Holfield read about Witig's suicide in the newspaper—a gunshot to the head while mountain climbing—when he didn't get the approval his company was counting on for the blockbuster drug, Juvena, purported to cure aging.

Inger Kroll, Witig's administrative assistant and ex-lover, was left with nothing but memories. When Holfield bumped into the attractive blonde at the funeral, he struck up a conversation.

"Don't I know you?" Paul asked.

"You should," Inger answered. "I arranged for your meeting with Witig before you left the company. I even wired your bonus to the Swiss bank for you."

"Of course, you are Inger, but something is different about you."

"Just cut my hair. It's the same Inger except for that."

"How are you getting on without Rolfe? Such a tragic end to a brilliant career," Holfield had lied.

"Well, with what little is left of the company up for sale, I suppose I'll be looking for a new job."

Holfield eyed her and then said, "Why look any further when you can come and work for me?"

Inger took him up on the offer, and thus a new relationship was born. She moved from Zurich to Bern and began her new role as Paul Holfield's administrative assistant. It didn't take long before the two were engaging in after-hour liaisons. Their relationship soon became an open affair, and Inger accompanied her new boss to most official functions. Holfield would introduce her as his "fiancée," but had no real intention of marriage. He just needed to satisfy corporate code.

When Inger first met Gustav Jung at a company dinner event, Holfield noticed him immediately light up. Inger was elegant, blond, tall, and curvaceous, and any normal man would look twice at her. Gustav turned to Paul when she wasn't looking to give him an approving nod and wink.

***

Holfield couldn't wait to satisfy his inner cravings. He left the hotel suite for a minute, found a private spot, and phoned his consort from days past who went by the name Natalie. Her generic message came on his cell phone. "This is Natalie." Paul's pulse quickened just hearing her voice. "Leave your name along with the time and place I should meet you and a name of the person who referred you. I listen to my messages frequently. If I can't make it, I will call back to reschedule. Otherwise expect to see me at the time and place you indicate."

He spoke into the phone. "Natalie, this is Paul Holfield. I'm a close friend of George Fleming, who referred me. I'm in town on business and would like to see you tonight at two a.m. I'll be in a suite at the Delano." Finishing his message, Holfield hung up.

It will be an expensive night, but well worth it, he thought.

Next he made the reservation. The Delano had its own private entrance separate from the more public Mandalay Bay, to which it was connected. He would pay in cash. That way Inger, who reviewed all his expenses, would never know about it.

When Paul returned to the Bellagio suite, Inger was prepared and waiting. She was wearing the slinky outfit he preferred, one that left little to the imagination. As soon as Paul entered, Inger was on him. She started undoing his tie and rubbing up against him.

Before things got hot and heavy, he told her, "Darling, I'd like to go out after dinner tonight to do a little gambling. You want to come with?" He anticipated her answer.

"Paul, you know how I hate the casinos. Even with their ventilation systems, they are always full of damned cigarette smoke. You go and have a good time. I'm still a little jet-lagged anyway, so getting to bed after dinner will do me good."

"I hope you're not too jet-lagged for this?" Paul bent down and kissed her neck while undoing her bra. His erection was practically staring her in the face.

"I'm never too tired for this," Inger said, laughing as she caressed his hardness, then putting her mouth and tongue to work on him.

Holfield closed his eyes and enjoyed. Ohhh, baby…that feels so good."

7

Gabe got a page from his secretary. "Dr. Schaeffer, there's a Lieutenant Holmes in the office to see you."

"Gee, I don't recall any meeting with a policeman scheduled for this afternoon." Gabe scratched his head.

"It's not a scheduled appointment, Dr. Schaeffer. The man is from the Defense Department and wants to speak with you about your research project."

Gabe thought fast. "Oh, it's probably about our OX312 work. We have a government grant funding it. Please ask Lieutenant Holmes to have a seat. I'll be over in a few minutes."

He left the research building and quickly headed to the fifth floor of the main hospital building, where the psychiatry department offices were located. As he walked through the door to his office, Gabe wondered about the reason for an unscheduled visit. He had meticulously filled out the documentation forms on his study for its midterm review. No one from Washington had ever come on an unscheduled site visit before.

"Lieutenant Holmes, I'm Gabriel Schaeffer," he said, extending his hand to greet the visitor.

Holmes shook his host's hand. "Let me apologize about the impromptu visit. I had other business in Boston and thought I'd stop by to discuss your project as long as I was in the vicinity."

"Sure. I'm glad you came by. In fact, if I recall correctly, we submitted our midterm report to your office only one week ago."

"Yes, and let me thank you for sending your report on time. Some of our investigators take their sweet time about forwarding the requested information, and it ends up giving me a big headache. On occasion, I've even had to send out an armed platoon to get those reports."

Gabe looked at Holmes with a surprised expression. "Oh, I'm just joking, Dr. Schaeffer," Holmes said. "Anyway, in all seriousness, our records show you have had Defense Department funding for the last two and a half years."

"That's correct."

"Our review committee has gone through your latest filing, which indicated that a statistically significant major endpoint has not been reached. Accordingly, it's my duty to let you know Defense will not be renewing your funding for another go-around. In fact, we must put an immediate hold on the project's research account."

"That can't be correct. Some of the most important work is still in progress."

"I'm sorry, Dr. Schaeffer, but this is the result of our current review, and the order to terminate has already been signed by my superior officer, Colonel Ferguson."

"I don't believe it. There must be some mistake."

"I can assure you, there has been no mistake. But please accept some advice. Try not to take this personally. Due to a significant decrease in our budget, other deserving research projects have been terminated as well."

Gabe was disappointed and confused.

Holmes had set the stage for his pitch. "There might be one option that could work for you."

"What's that?"

"The Defense Department would obtain rights for the OX312 you have been using in your project. In exchange, you will receive a one-time lump-sum payment of $250,000. That should take the sting out of the situation. With that much money at hand, you can find something else more interesting to research or perhaps take a nice, long vacation to the destination of your choice."

"Let me make sure I get this right, Lieutenant Holmes. The government is has stopped funding for our project but wants to buy rights to the drug? That makes no sense."

"Well, sir, all I can tell you is that it makes sense to someone with a higher rank than mine at the Defense Department. I might interject that I have personally reviewed the proposal at length and think the offer is very fair."

"I don't know. I'm in the middle…"

"Dr. Schaeffer, let me suggest you take a day or two to think about it? Perhaps a little time is needed to help you see that our offer is the best solution, given your situation."

Gabe was speechless; he really didn't know how to respond. Holmes stood up to leave. "Feel free to contact me anytime. Otherwise, you can expect a callback in the next few days."

Holmes put his business card with contact information on Gabe's desk, then turned and walked out the door.

Gabe sat at his desk in a state of shock. It just didn't add up. But the money Holmes offered was much more than Gabe made in salary during a whole year. It certainly would make terminating the research project more palatable, or would it? He had spent the last two years working with the OX312 drug, and now that it looked like it had a positive impact on preventing violent behavior, was it right to quit? How may untold lives could OX312 save if it worked as well as his research suggested?

He came to a quick decision. There was no way he would accept Holmes's offer or any other, regardless of the amount. He knew Angela would agree, but he had to tell her about what had just transpired. After all, the drug was rightfully hers. She was the one who had modified the oxytocin peptide in the first place to give it the unique properties OX312 possessed. That said, what was he going to do for continued funding? As he sat there in his office, Gabe had no idea where the money he needed to continue their research would come from.

8

Gabe went to meet Angela at the Yankee Clipper for dinner. Explaining the Defense Department canceled their research funding was not going to be fun.

He sat at a table nursing a glass of Chardonnay, waiting for Angela to arrive. Gabe was thinking of how best to break the bad news to her. She saw him after entering the door and went over to his table.

"Hey, Angela, glad you could make it."

"Sorry I'm a little late. Had a few extra things to finish up at the lab before leaving. I have to tell you, I'm really excited about the couples' therapy study using OX312. To date I have six enrolled, and the results are looking promising. None have quit coming to sessions, and all are reporting positive results in communication and sexual relations."

"Terrific. I'm glad to hear that." Gabe said, then his face took on a sad look as he continued. "Angela, I have some news to share with you regarding the OX312 research, and I'm afraid you won't like it."

"What's the matter?" Angela asked.

"It's about funding. The Defense Department is terminating our grant.

"But in God's name, why would they do that? Our work is showing such positive results."

"I understand, but I guess they must have their reasons. An officer, Lieutenant Holmes, from the section responsible for our funding met with me. The odd thing was that although Holmes told me they can't continue supporting our research, he offered to buy rights to OX312. I refused to sell on your behalf. Hope you don't mind."

"Of course I don't mind. You know how important this project is to me."

***

Gabe knew Angela was totally dedicated to her research using OX312, but he didn't know one of the major driving forces behind it. That had a lot to do with the vicious fighting between her parents she witnessed as a child. Her father was a brilliant man who immigrated to the United States with his wife and child when Angela was only a baby. He worked his way up the academic ladder, receiving a doctorate in mathematics from Berkeley and later becoming chairman of the department.

In spite of his brilliance, Dr. Chen had a taste for *baijiu*, a favorite drink otherwise known as 'Chinese vodka'. He told friends it helped him feel connected with the homeland he left behind. However, Chen's consumption increased over time, and his behavior deteriorated, resulting in him losing his position at the university. With too much free time on his hands, the only mathematical equation that concerned him was getting enough money to buy his daily quota of baijiu.

The problem led to frequent battles at home. Angela could still see her father with a belt in his hand, chasing her mother around the house. He was always screaming for her to give him money, then beating her until she was left a whimpering heap lying on the floor. Angela was powerless to physically intervene, so she would lock herself in the bedroom and call 911. It was a pattern that repeated itself all too often which ended with her father being led away in handcuffs. Angela's mother's foolish pride and devotion kept her from ever filing charges.

The fighting only stopped when Chen developed liver cancer due to his excessive drinking, and he became too weak to get out of bed. It didn't take long for the cancer to ravage his alcohol-weakened body and kill him. The last thing Angela remembered him telling her when he briefly came out of coma was in Cantonese, "*Yui di yat bui mh'goi.*" *One more cup please.* Angela was sixteen at the time, and her father's behavior left her with a desperate longing for peace and stability in her life.

Angela Chen's research into the biological mechanisms of violence held a very special meaning for her…a meaning she wasn't ready to fully share with anyone, even Gabe Schaffer, the man she worked so closely with and adored. If she could understand the biological root of violent behavior, then there was a chance to figure out how to control what had so unsettled her during youth and help prevent others from experiencing similar trauma.

***

"I know it means the world to you," Gabe said.

"What are we going to do to keep our projects up and running?"

"I can guarantee you that I'll find a solution. Boston General has its own research foundation, and I will apply tomorrow for emergency funding. After that I'll submit for an NIH grant, and I think there is an excellent chance for getting approval, although that could take several months." Gabe thought for a moment, then continued. "Look, both of us already have positive findings in our clinical studies, so instead of gloom and doom, let's celebrate tonight. What do you say, Angela?"

The despondent look on her face quickly subsided, and she answered, "I say why not?"

"Great!" Gabe exclaimed, as he motioned the waiter over. "I'll have another one of these," he said, pointing to his empty Chardonnay glass. "Angela, what would you like?"

"Hmm, I think I'll go with a Diet Coke and a lime. I don't drink alcohol."

"OK, a Diet Coke for the lady and don't forget the lime."

They ate dinner, laughed, and danced to the music the band was playing. For the time being, both forgot about their concerns regarding funding. When they parted and went their separate ways, it was near midnight.

On his way home from the Yankee Clipper, Gabe noticed he couldn't get Angela off his mind. He was struck by an intense desire to see and be with her again. Gabe started visualizing Angela without clothes on. He saw himself running his hand up one of her long smooth legs, reaching up to the soft warmth between her thighs. Gabe felt himself getting erect.

Instead of continuing home, he turned around and headed for Angela's place. Gabe called her on his cell.

"Angela, I know it's late and this might sound crazy, but I need to see you right away. Can I come over?"

"Of course," she answered. "I was hoping you would call."

"I'll be there in ten minutes," Gabe said, his heart beating faster in anticipation as he picked up his stride.

When he entered her apartment, as Gabe was about to speak, she put her index finger up to his lips as if to shush him and said, "I know." Then she threw her arms around his neck, kissing him deeply. In moments they were naked, making love on the carpet of her living room. Angela moaned in ecstasy. This was what she had dreamed about for so long.

Gabe had no thought of the ramifications of his actions. He unabashedly explored every part of Angela's body, enraptured. Their voracious lovemaking lasted until both finally collapsed from sheer fatigue.

When Gabe awoke early the next morning, he opened his eyes and saw Angela's naked body next to his. Suddenly, Gabe was panic stricken, realizing he had broken his cardinal rule regarding professional behavior: no sexual relations with a work colleague. *Oh God, what have I done?*

Gabe tried to make sense of it. He only had two glasses of wine at dinner, so Gabe couldn't blame the alcohol. Angela was pretty, intelligent, and had a wonderful body. She was everything Gabe wanted in a woman. Under other circumstances he would have liked nothing better than to have sex with her. However, they were working as colleagues on major research projects. A relationship that went beyond a strictly professional one was out of the question.

He slithered out of the bed and picked up his clothes. Tiptoeing out of the bedroom, he dressed in the living room so as not to disturb her sleep. His heart was pounding, but not because of desire. Now it was because of anxiety about the implications of allowing his unrestrained lust to get the better of him with a work associate.

Gabe opened the door of Angela's apartment and left, wondering how he was ever going to face her again.

Later that day, Gabe confronted Angela at the lab, and she could tell he was embarrassed. With a flushed face, Gabe said, "Angela, about last night, I don't know what to tell you. Something came over me, I'm not sure what. But I have to apologize. It can't be allowed to happen again. We both have way too much at stake in the work we do to let a physical relationship develop between us."

Angela wished Gabe didn't want to pull back from what she yearned for so desperately, but what choice did she have? Angela wanted Gabe to love her, but couldn't tell him about the dose of OX312 she put in his drink when he wasn't looking, or the small amount she took to give herself the courage to act. He would never forgive her for that. So she decided it best to acquiesce.

"Sure, Gabe, I totally agree with you. It will never happen again."

9

Holmes phoned Gabe two days later from his office in Washington.

"Well, since I haven't heard from you," he told Gabe, "I thought it would be a good idea for me to call and listen to what you have to say about my offer." Holmes already had a good sense the answer would be no.

"Sorry I didn't get back to you," Gabe told him, "but I can't in good conscience sell you rights to the drug."

"Dr. Schaeffer, you realize the funding for your projects has been frozen."

"Yes, and I wish you hadn't done that."

"Your decision to say no is final?"

"Yes, final."

"What if I sweetened up our offer a bit? Let's say up to three hundred and fifty thousand dollars."

"Sorry, Lieutenant Holmes, but no there is no price we are willing to sell at."

"Then there isn't anything further to discuss. Let me wish you good luck and say good-bye."

As he got off the line, Holmes was thinking Ferguson was not going to be happy learning the results of his conversation with Schaeffer. He needed to come up with some way to make absolutely sure Schaeffer's research would end.

Holmes put in a call to his boss. "No luck, sir. Schaeffer didn't go for the extra cash."

"Well, it seems that son of a bitch doesn't realize it's not smart to fuck with Uncle Sam," Ferguson said. "Why don't you go to Boston, and see what you can personally do to resolve the situation? Catch my drift?"

"Yes sir, I understand."

***

Holmes stared at himself in the mirror of his hotel room while wearing a white lab coat. He added a pair of glasses, hung a stethoscope around his neck, and was ready to go play doctor.

The lieutenant entered the Boston General Research Building at eight o'clock in the evening, after most of the staff had gone home. Holmes knew the exact location of where he was going, to Schaeffer's lab, where he planned on stealing the hard drives to their computers. They would then have to start their research over from scratch and do it with no obvious funding. That would be certain to kill all their current projects and the drug's future development.

He picked open the lab's locked door in moments. Once inside, Holmes started working at the computer on Gabe's desk. He removed four bolts, and the back of the computer came off. Holmes would have the first hard drive in his hand in minutes. *This job is a piece of cake*, he thought.

But things didn't go as planned. When he heard a noise at the door, Holmes quickly ducked under the desk and waited.

Angela came back to the office after a late dinner to review data. She went over to her desk and sat down. Before she knew what happened, someone was on her. He grabbed her from behind and held her mouth so she couldn't scream.

"Just be quiet, and no harm will come to you." Angela was trembling. "I want you to lie down on the floor. I'm going to tape your hands and put some over your mouth. You won't get hurt if you cooperate."

She was shocked. Who would do this?

Angela pulled her head away and tried to scream, "Hel—" Before she could finish her plea for assistance he again placed his hand over her mouth. Then Angela bit him hard. She heard her attacker say, "Goddamn it." Then he hit her on the back of the head. Angela saw stars and went limp.

When she came to, the man was gone. Angela felt a tender lump on the back of her head, then saw her fingers covered with fresh blood.

"Oh shit," she said aloud. He had hit her hard enough to cause a laceration to her scalp. Perhaps she needed stitches, but first Angela had to call Gabe.

She picked up the phone, and called, waking him from a sound sleep. Angela was sobbing. "Gabe, I was attacked in the lab. A man hit me over the head and knocked me out."

"Are you OK?" He didn't wait for her answer. "I'm coming over. You just stay put. I'll be there in a few minutes."

Angela went over to the sink and looked in the mirror. She washed the blood off her face and then went to the ice machine, filling a plastic bag and placing it over the swollen area on her scalp. Sitting on the sofa, she waited for Gabe to arrive. A minute later, he flew through the door and saw Angela.

"Are you all right?" he asked, breathless from running.

"I'll be fine," she said. "I'm more angry than hurt at this point."

"Here, let me look." He worked through her hair, matted with blood.

"I must look like hell," she said.

"Don't worry about how you look. There's only a small gash, and it isn't bleeding any longer. Luckily, I don't think you'll need stitches. Maybe I should take you over to the emergency room and get a CT scan of your head."

"I'll be fine. If you think I'm going to spend the rest of the night in an ER, you're *crazy*." Then she added, "Oops, I probably shouldn't have used that word, especially with you."

"Very funny," Gabe said.

He looked through the office and found nothing was stolen. Then Gabe noticed his computer had been tampered with. The back cover was off.

"It looks like whoever did this was after the hard drives," Gabe said. "Did you get a look at him?"

"No. He was behind me, so I never saw his face."

"Well, I think this whole thing must have something to do with the refusal to sell our OX312. Somebody was trying to help himself to all our data and screw us over by stealing it."

"Gabe, we should call the police."

"If we do that, you can kiss our research projects good-bye forever. If news about tonight gets out, we'll never find anyone to fund us." He thought for a moment. "The thing to do now is keep quiet, and hope they leave us alone. I have the card with a phone number for Lieutenant Holmes, the man who visited from Washington. He's probably knows who was behind this. I'll call tomorrow and tell him any more funny business, and we go straight to the police. They won't dare attempt anything again."

"I hope you're right, Gabe. This was pretty scary."

"I know I'm right," he said, trying to sound confident.

Gabe drove Angela home and walked her up to the apartment. "Sleep late and don't come in tomorrow. Take the day off to recover."

"Don't be ridiculous. I'm not going to let a little bump on the head keep me from my work. Just do me one great favor. Please stay over tonight. I don't think I will get any rest unless you do."

"Well…"

As Gabe hesitated, Angela added, "Don't worry. You can sleep on my sofa in the living room. I just don't want to be alone in the apartment tonight."

"Sure, you're right. I'll stay."

Gabe walked up the stairs to her apartment. Going inside brought back memories of the passion he had let loose the last time there. As he lay on Angela's sofa trying to fall asleep, he remembered her soft breasts pressed against his chest, and her silky legs wrapped around his body. Gabe shook his head to help the vision leave his brain. Then his thoughts turned to the serious predicament they found themselves in. He vowed to get to the bottom of what was going on.

10

After dinner at the Bellagio's best restaurant, Paul led Inger to the elevators, and kissed her good-night. She headed up to their room, while he marched straight to the blackjack tables. Over the next few hours, Paul made his gambling rounds, which included visits to the Caesars and Wynn. After that, he got into a limo which drove him to his final destination, the Delano at Mandalay Bay. By then the Novara executive was up nearly twenty thousand in winnings and feeling pretty good.

Holfield sat alone in the suite awaiting his special guest. The doorbell rang at precisely 2:00 a.m. He got up and opened the door. Natalie stood there in a tight-fitting dress with a low-cut front. She had long jet-black hair very different from the short-cut red hair he recalled from their last encounter.

"Mr. Holfield."

"Yes, and aren't you punctual," he observed, looking down at his watch.

"I don't like to keep my friends waiting."

"Please come in."

Natalie carried a stylish Fendi leather backpack slung across her shoulder. "I brought some refreshments along," she said, pulling out a bottle of chilled Cristal champagne. A set of fluted glasses followed. She poured the bubbling golden liquid and handed one of the glasses to Paul.

As he took a sip, she asked, "Don't I know you?"

"What makes you say that?"

"That accent of yours, it's British. I'm sure I've heard it before, and not just from the call you made on my voice mail."

"Well, can you keep a secret?"

"Of course, honey. I do my job for you, and no one else ever knows. Absolute privacy is part of what you are paying for."

"OK then. Do you remember George Fleming?"

"The reference you gave? It's you, isn't it? You're George."

"Yes."

"What happened? Your voice is the same, but the face, it's completely different."

"I sure as hell hope so. I paid an awful lot of money to the surgeon who did this for me, and even told him to make me look a little better. Did he succeed?" Holfield asked gleefully.

"If I remember correctly, you didn't look so bad before. Why did you have the surgery? Were you in an accident?"

"Not an accident. Just got in a jam and had to change my appearance and name. Now the old George is dead, and a new Paul lives on."

"Enough talk, let's get you comfortable." Natalie began methodically taking off his clothes. She rubbed his crotch with one hand while she unbuckled his belt with the other. When he was naked, with his erection in front of her, she pretended to closely examine his penis as if she were his urologist.

"You're George Fleming all right. I could never forget a cock this big." Both of them laughed as they took another sip of champagne. George swallowed his and sighed.

"Ah, that's good champagne."

Natalie didn't say anything. While her mouth still held the champagne, she engulfed his hardness. The effervescence of the bubbles and the movements of her tongue drove Paul mad.

"That's the Natalie I remember!" he exclaimed. Soon he was groaning in ecstasy, moving his hips back and forth to match her tempo. At the right moment, Natalie stopped and brought her head up from between his legs.

"I'll be back in a moment," she said. "I need to get into something comfortable."

"Hurry back," he gruffly ordered as she grabbed her tote bag and took off for the bathroom.

"I won't be but a moment," she called back, closing the door behind her.

Natalie quickly got out of her clothes and left herself wearing only a G-string. She reached into her bag and bought out a vial containing white powder. Carefully she poured some onto the granite sink top, lined it, then inhaled deeply along its length. Afterward she paused to enjoy the rush. Natalie wiped her nose clean and primped her hair in the mirror. She pinched her nipples to get them erect, then headed back out to her client.

"OK, George, Paul, or whatever you want your name to be—Natalie is ready to play."

11

Holmes reported to Ferguson at his DC office. "There has been no police report filed since the incident with Dr. Chen at the Boston General Research lab."

"That's interesting," Ferguson said.

Holmes offered his opinion. "They probably don't want to draw attention to their project while still having to scrounge around for funding."

"That may be true, but we're still back at square one. We don't have the drug in our possession."

"You know, that Asian bitch was pretty tough. She wasn't going to cooperate no matter what and practically bit my finger off." Holmes held up his bandaged left hand.

"Maybe using force isn't the way to get what we want." Ferguson was thinking. After a pause he continued. "I'm going to call a friend of mine at the CIA. He's someone who specializes in the kind of tactics a situation like this calls for."

After their meeting ended and Holmes left the office, Ferguson placed a call to the agency and asked for William Mueller.

"Bill, it's your buddy, Scott Ferguson."

"Hey, you old horse's ass, how are you?"

"If I was any better, I'd think I was dead and gone to heaven."

"You aren't going to end up there, no matter what. It's the other place you're headed for." They laughed, then Mueller went on. "If I remember correctly, weren't you supposed to take me out for a round of golf at the Army Navy Country Club in Arlington about a year ago?"

"Good memory, but you know how things go. I've been up to my neck in work and haven't had time to hit the links."

"Sure, sure, I know," Mueller said. "We're all working harder and getting paid less. So what can I do for you?"

"Bit of a problem that I could use your assistance with."

"Lay it on me."

"There's this doctor, Gabriel Schaeffer, and his research assistant, Angela Chen, in Boston. They are working with a drug that renders highly violent criminals harmless. In fact, it makes them so downright friendly, they wouldn't hurt a fly. Defense originally funded their research but came to the conclusion we don't want any more work done on that agent. Our belief is that the drug could pose a threat to national security."

"How is that?"

"Well, what if our enemies got their hands on it and figured out a way to administer it to our troops? They could turn our toughest marines into a bunch of pussies. Now, that would be a hell of a weapon. Catch my drift?"

"What can I do to help?"

"Well, we offered to buy rights to the drug, and Schaeffer refused. Then there was an unfortunate physical confrontation with his female colleague when Holmes, my attaché, tried to lift their computer hard drives. Chen turned out to be a feisty little bitch, and it seems intimidation or force isn't going to work with these folks. That's why I'm calling you. You've got the best brains in the spook business. Do you think you can help us?"

Mueller thought about the story he just heard. *So they have a drug that works like magic, turning vicious criminals into nice guys... guys you'd want to have a beer with."* He was silent for a moment, then spoke. "Tell you what. If I take care of this matter for you, can the agency have the drug?"

"Sure, better you than the Russians or Chinese. But why would the CIA want it?"

"Maybe our boys at Gitmo could find it useful. Ever since water-boarding has been banned, they've been looking for a new way to get the asshole terrorists telling us what we want to know. Playing loud rock music and keeping them awake for days on end just doesn't cut it. Getting one of those jihadists talking could save scores of lives by giving us the info we need to prevent a major attack. A drug that works like the one you're telling me about could make a big difference in dealing with those bastards. Shit, maybe we could even arrange to sprinkle a little of it on the Russian foreign minister's breakfast cereal when he visits the White House. By lunchtime he'd agree with anything we wanted."

"Well, that approach might not go over big with our commander in chief," Ferguson said.

"Who says the commander in chief would even know about it? We agency people sometimes keep things strictly to ourselves." They chuckled as Mueller went on. "So here's the deal on the drug. If I get the job done, you'll let us have it."

"Sure. You guys get it, and it's is all yours."

"Then we've got a deal?"

"You have my verbal signature on the dotted line."

"Great."

"I'll be sending you a secure e-mail with the particulars shortly. But before I get off, can I ask how you intend to do this?"

"Hey, I don't ask you how you do your job. Do I? Anyway, I'll keep you in the loop."

"Thanks, Bill."

"It's always a pleasure to help out a friend. The agency is here for Defense whenever you need us."

"Later."

Mueller added one last item. "You still owe me that golf game, and I'm holding you to it."

"OK. I'll send you a tee-off time when I send my e-mail with the details."

Later that day Mueller opened the message from Ferguson and read through it. Along with a tee-off time at the Army Navy Country Club was the additional information:

"Dr. Gabriel Schaeffer is a forty-two-year-old bachelor. He is a graduate of Harvard Medical. Currently he practices psychiatry at Boston General and has a specialty in dealing with the violent criminal mind. He works with an Asian research assistant, Angela Chen, and together they developed the drug we spoke about, OX312..." As Mueller continued reading through the information, he thought, *I have just the person to get the damn drug without breaking any bones.*

Mueller planned to contact one of his best operatives, someone with a proven track record of successes. He had no doubt Pamela Carter could pull this one off.

12

She spoke softly to her father. "Hi Daddy, I just wanted to drop by and visit with you."

Pamela scanned the area around her, then said, "What a gorgeous day. The sun is out, and there's a nice breeze coming off the Potomac. It makes me want to lie down and take a nap right here next to you."

She knelt down, placing a small bouquet against the headstone that read:

Bernard Carter
Col US Army
Vietnam
Desert Storm
Operation Enduring Freedom
8/2/1956—6/4/2008

Pamela's frequent missions didn't give her much time stateside, but when in DC, she always went to her father's grave at Arlington. A career soldier who served as a Green Beret in Vietnam, her father had also distinguished himself on later tours of duty in Iraq and Afghanistan. It wasn't a bullet that took his life, but an unstoppable pancreatic cancer. Her mother died when she was too young to remember. Pamela grew up the consummate military brat, accompanying her father from base to base or temporarily sent to her aunt's when he headed off for war.

Her last mission over, Pamela was in DC awaiting the next assignment. As she left the cemetery, her phone went off.

"Pam, Mueller here."

"Yes sir."

"Gotten a good rest since Berlin?"

"Yes sir. I really needed it."

"Terrific. Wanted to let you know we have a new job waiting for you."

"Where am I off to this time?"

"You're going all the way to Boston."

"Boston? Let me guess. You want me to pick up a couple of fresh lobsters and bring them back to you?"

"As a matter of fact I am allergic to lobster, but I'm not kidding. This assignment is a domestic matter that has important security implications for our country."

"Oh?"

"The good thing about the job from your standpoint is that nobody will be shooting at you. You might even find it a bit of a vacation. Boston isn't a bad place to hang out for a few weeks. Stop by my office at fourteen hundred hours and I'll give you the details in person."

"To be honest, I like the idea of no bullets. That would be a welcome change."

"This assignment calls for your brains and feminine charm, but not guns."

Pamela chuckled. "If I recall correctly you said the same thing about Berlin. 'No guns.' I don't like to criticize my superiors, but you were way off the mark on that one."

"Come on, Pam, cut me some slack. Who knew Rahmani would want to pocket the money we gave him and try stealing the gyros to boot? Nobody could have seen that coming."

"Well I'll give you a pass on Berlin. I never figured on what was going to happen either. Anyway, see you later on this afternoon."

***

Pam remembered the Berlin mission she had just completed. The agency had turned a German citizen of Mideast origin, a man named Mansur, who was in the business of exporting high technology military equipment to the highest bidder. The agency had him set up a sale of advanced gyro systems, intended for Iranian ballistic missiles, to an attaché working at their embassy. The Iranians were full of bluster about their weapons systems but way short on know-how. They had to buy just about every component on the black market.

Rahmani was the Iranian agent in Berlin who pretended to be a diplomat, and did most of their component acquisitions. What he didn't know was that the gyros were flawed and actually made to fail. The CIA was going to use Mansur to pass along bad equipment to Rahmani. Nothing pleased the agency people at Langley more than the thought of Iranian missiles flying off in every direction except toward their intended targets.

Mansur had arranged for Rahmani to meet him in a hotel suite, and consummate the deal. The Iranian brought along a briefcase filled with deutsche marks and Mansur a box full of gyros, which lay open on the coffee table in front of him. Pam was present, dressed in a slinky black cocktail dress with stiletto high heels. She spoke fluent German, and appeared every bit the mistress to Mansur, which had been her role in the charade.

"Can I offer you a drink?" Pam had politely asked Rahmani after he arrived.

"Sure. A scotch would be nice."

"You drink alcohol?" Mansur had asked, looking surprised.

"And why not? I'm a good Muslim when in Tehran, but in Berlin…well, in Berlin I do as I damn well please."

"I totally understand," Mansur had said with an empathetic tone, giving Rahmani a wink at the same time. "Luckily, as a Christian, I don't have those ludicrous restrictions when visiting home in Lebanon. We have no morality police chasing our women around and whipping them if they aren't wearing hijabs and floor-length dresses. Then smiling and taking a sip of his own vodka tonic, Mansur added, "And we can drink whatever we want just like here, in Berlin."

"Those fucking *morality* police, they make me sick. Most of them are goddamned pedophiles."

Mansur chuckled at Rahmani's vehement put-down of the fanatic Islamists that infested his homeland.

Pam had placed the drink she prepared in front of Rahmani, bending down to do so, and giving him a view of her breasts in the process. Their guest lifted his glass and took a drink.

"Here are the gyro guidance mechanisms as you requested," Mansur said, extending his hand toward an open box sitting on the cocktail table.

"May I ask where you got them?"

"My dear friend, I have spent years cultivating the sources I use. Let's be honest. You'd cut me out in a minute if I told you where they came from. The important thing is that they are here in front of you just as we agreed. Now that I've shown you mine, please show me yours."

Rahmani had opened the briefcase he brought along. "Here are the five hundred thousand deutsche marks as you requested, and many thanks from Tehran."

While Mansur focused on the money, Rahmani had pulled out his gun with a silencer from the waistband behind his back and shot his host square in the forehead. Mansur's head had jolted back with a snap as the back of his skull blew apart, splattering fragments onto the wall behind. Rahmani nonchalantly got up from his seat and locked both the briefcase containing the money and the box with the gyros. Next he had turned to Pam and spoke to her as if nothing dramatic had occurred.

"Tomorrow this money will be deposited in my bank account in Zurich. It seems I got the gyros free of charge, and that is what I call a good deal!" With a smile he politely asked, "Perhaps you would like to become my girlfriend now that Mansur has left us?

Before she had time to answer Rahmani had brusquely ordered, "Now take off your clothes."

Pam had pretended to be scared, allowing Rahmani to feel in charge. She got up from her seat and did as told. Unzipping her dress, Pam let it fall to the floor. She had stood in front of the cold-blooded murderer clad only in her bra and skimpy panties.

"Come on, take the rest off. You don't need to be shy with me." She undid her bra and tossed it to the side so her breasts were exposed, then slid off her panties. Rahmani's eyes had widened. "Beautiful! When we are done, I'll give you a thousand marks, then we'll go out somewhere nice for dinner. That's more money than that Mansur would have given you. Am I not correct?"

Pam didn't answer but had no doubt she wouldn't leave the hotel room alive after Rahmani had his pleasure with her.

As he had stood admiring her body, she bent down to remove her high heels. Pam slipped off the first one and stepped down. Next her second shoe came off.

In a split second, she had exploded upward, forcing Rahmani's hand away and causing the gun to discharge harmlessly into the ceiling. With her other hand holding the shoe she had just removed, Pamela had crammed its six-inch stiletto heel deep into his eye socket. Rahmani let out a hellish scream of pain mixed with surprise, then had fallen backward onto the bed with the shoe's heel impaled in his brain. His body stiffened for a few moments, then went limp. Ramani was dead.

***

Mueller had been wrong about Berlin, but Pam was an experienced operative prepared for the unexpected. In fact, she relished the element of surprise that challenged her abilities to their fullest. On the other hand, a brief respite with the stateside mission her boss proposed would be welcome. *A easy assignment in Boston,* she thought. *I guess that's his way of being nice to me after what happened in Berlin.*

13

The day after meeting with Mueller, Pamela Carter paid the first visit to the agency library and started reading everything she could get her hands on regarding the psychology of violent behavior. After a week of around-the-clock preparation, she was ready to put her newfound knowledge into action. Pam phoned the department of psychiatry at Boston General and asked, "May I speak with Dr. Gabriel Schaeffer?"

When he came on the line, she introduced herself. "Hello, Dr. Schaeffer, this is Vanessa Trent, a graduate student in psychology. You don't know me, but I am a great admirer of your work. I wonder if it would be possible for me to visit Boston General and spend the next four weeks observing on your clinical service."

"What are you doing now?"

"I'm working on my master's thesis in the department of psychology at Walter Reed under Dr. Karl Heffner. He highly recommended working with you. In fact, Dr. Heffner told me you're the authority when it comes to understanding violence, and that's my special area of interest."

***

Mueller had helped to carefully set up the cover for his agent. He contacted Heffner at Walter Reed National Military Medical Center and assured him of the importance of the mission to national security. Without providing details Mueller filled him in on his plans of an agent posing as someone working under him. Heffner had once served in the PSYOPs, psychological operations branch of the CIA. He readily agreed to help out in any way he could, and without asking questions.

***

"Of course I know Dr. Heffner, at least through his writings. I've read his papers on the origins of religious fanaticism and terrorism. He's clearly one of the best in the field. You are very fortunate to have a mentor held in such high regard. Sure, it would be my pleasure if you came to do a rotation here at Boston General."

"Thanks so much, Dr. Schaeffer."

"Do you have somewhere to stay? If not, my secretary, Mary Ann, can help you with arrangements."

"No, that won't be necessary, but I appreciate the offer."

"Well, why don't I transfer your call to Mary Ann? She will give you the details of our schedule and help make arrangements for getting your ID badge after arriving."

"That's so kind of you, Dr. Schaeffer."

"Hopefully, you can start at Boston General first thing next week."

"Yes, and I very much look forward to seeing you. Thanks again."

Sounds like such a nice person, Gabe thought after transferring her call to his secretary. He had no way of knowing it then, but the agency operative had acted over the phone in precisely the manner her mission warranted. For the time being, Pam Carter was going to try hooking her target, Gabriel Schaeffer, by playing the sweet but brainy, girl-next-door type.

***

Pamela studied textbooks on neurobiology and psychopathology, learning them inside and out. Focusing on criminal violence, Pamela read every one of Gabriel Schaeffer's published papers on the topic. No doubt she had personally been involved in some rather violent activities herself, but only in service to her country.

As a child she accompanied her proud father around the army base and learned how to properly salute before she spoke in sentences. There was nothing more Pamela loved more as a little girl than sitting on her father's lap and listening to his stories of battle and heroism. In school she excelled in academics as well as sports. Pamela beat the boys in most things. After her mother died when Pam was turning four, her father never remarried.

By the time of Colonel Carter's death from cancer, Pam was well on the way to fulfilling her own dreams of service to country. She had an IQ that was off the charts and a photographic memory to boot. Those abilities allowed her to learn just about anything she put her mind to quickly and with proficiency. In addition, by adding some makeup and the right kind of clothing, she could morph into a strikingly gorgeous vixen able to turn the head of any man.

Pamela joined the agency after graduating with honors from The Citadel. She was observed and tested extensively, then chosen to begin training in covert operations. Her dad had put his life on the line many times, proudly wearing the battle scars and medals to prove it. For Pam Carter, like for her old man, it was now her turn to serve.

On her desk lay the file on Dr. Gabriel Schaeffer. It contained everything of importance about his life from birth until now. She still had plenty of homework to do before beginning at Boston General on Monday. As she thumbed through Schaeffer's information, Pamela Carter had no doubt that about getting him to give the agency his OX312, and that she could accomplish her mission just as Mueller ordered, without breaking any bones.

14

Angela saw Gabe sitting in the hospital cafeteria and ran over to his table. "Gabe, I'm so glad I ran into you. I have some great news."

"What's that?"

"I just had my abstract on OX312 accepted! They've invited me to give an oral presentation at the upcoming meeting of the New England Society of Neurobiology."

"That's fantastic," Gabe said.

"It sure is. I'm so excited. The meeting is being held in New Haven next week. I'll drive down over the weekend. My presentation is scheduled for Wednesday. I can't wait. It should be a terrific conference." She paused a moment. "Gabe, it would be even better if you came along."

"I'd love to go, Angela, but I'm up to my neck in work. Plus, I'm still trying to hunt down the financial support needed for our projects. Our emergency funding won't be around much longer."

"I understand," she said with disappointment written on her face.

"But I expect you to knock 'em dead when you give your talk."

"Thanks. By the way, the abstract has been published over the Internet. You can read it online if you want."

"Well, I'm looking forward to doing that, just as soon as I get a free minute."

"Let me know what you think, will you? I could use some critical input before I leave."

"Of course I will. Go to the meeting and enjoy yourself. You deserve some time off, and please don't worry about a thing. I'll mind the lab while you're away."

"I hope you'll reconsider coming with," she said.

Gabe had no idea how much Angela wanted him to change his mind and say yes.

***

While in Vegas, Holfield's negotiations with representatives from several American pharmaceutical companies were proceeding as he planned. Holfield was also getting the most out of his trip in ways other than just business. During his free time Holfield visited his favorite dining and gambling haunts which helped make the long trip from Switzerland even more worthwhile. Having Inger available at his beckoning added to his enjoyment. After the clandestine meeting with Natalie, Holfield couldn't possibly have asked for more.

Each morning his work day would begin when he reviewed a memo, transmitted from the home office, covering topics of importance. This day Holfield got notice about several promising new drugs in the early stages of development.

As he sat sipping his morning cup of coffee, there was one inclusion that grabbed him. It was the title of an abstract from a scientific meeting about to take place in New Haven:

OX312, it's effect on rat social behavior indicating action as a 'love potion' and implications for use in humans; A. Chen PhD, G. Schaeffer MD, Neurobiology Research Laboratory, Boston General Hospital.

Holfield chuckled when he read the abstract's title nearly spilling his cup of coffee and awakening Inger, who was still asleep. Then his thoughts turned serious. *Someone believes they have a love potion for rats. But, what if it worked in humans? That could be something big... very big. I've got to make a stop in New Haven on the way back to Bern and listen to this presentation for myself.*

15

When Gabe entered his office early Monday morning, Vanessa was already sitting there waiting for him.

"You're here bright and early," Gabe said. She turned to look up at him.

"Well, I guess I am a little type A, but Mary Ann told me, 'the earlier the better.'"

Gabe was immediately blown away by her stunning beauty.

"Vanessa, isn't that correct?"

"Yes."

"Gabriel Schaeffer. I'm glad to meet you."

She stood up, gracefully extended her hand, holding on to his for a moment longer than he expected.

"I see you're dressed and ready for action." Vanessa was wearing the white lab coat Mary Ann had obtained for her, and had on a Boston General ID tag with her photo clipped to the front.

Vanessa pointed to the tag. "Oh, that's thanks to Mary Ann. She's been so helpful. I came to the hospital at the crack of dawn and got quickly processed through security."

"Terrific," Gabe said. "Can I offer you some coffee or tea before we get started? Our schedule today begins at the outpatient clinic."

"No thank you. I've already had a double shot of Starbucks on the way here."

"Well, if you're any kind of discriminating coffee drinker, you probably won't like the mud we serve here." Gabe poured himself a cup. "How was the trip from DC?"

"It was pretty smooth. Jumped on the commuter Saturday morning and got settled in."

"As I mentioned over the phone, if you should need anything, just let Mary Ann or me know. Here, let me give you my cell number just in case."

"Thanks, I appreciate that," Vanessa said, adding the digits he recited into her phone contacts.

As they spoke, Vanessa was checking out Gabe's office, looking at anything that might give her additional insights into his personality. It was one thing to read a file about someone and another to make an assessment in the flesh.

A dozen plaques hung on the wall behind Schaeffer's desk. She noted certifications in psychiatry and neurology. There was a PhD in neurobiology from Harvard, and a medical school diploma from John Hopkins. There was an award as best teacher of the year from the medical residents at Boston General. *He's all about his academics*, Vanessa thought. *That's what makes this guy tick.*

She noticed something that didn't quite fit with the other things mounted on the wall and asked, "Isn't that a picture of the Dalai Lama up there?"

"Yes, that was a gift from my research associate, Angela Chen. She is a devoted follower of the Dali Lama and his message of world peace. Angela is attending a conference in New Haven this week. I think you'll find her quite informative. If you have any questions about neurobiology of the brain, she's the one to ask."

Vanessa nodded her head in agreement, but inside she was thinking, *Knowledgeable on neurobiology but naïve about the world. The Dali Lama may want world peace, but it will take a lot more than prayer to save him and his Tibetan people from complete domination by the Chinese.*

Gabe finished off his coffee and threw the empty container into the trash. "Are you ready for the clinic?"

"I'm ready for anything," she answered.

Gabe stood and held the door open for Vanessa.

As she exited in front of him, Gabe couldn't help but notice her terrific legs.

16

The Novara private jet flew Paul and Inger from Vegas directly into New Haven. A limousine was waiting and whisked them off. Paul sat among the crowd attending the New England Neurobiology Conference when Angela Chen made her presentation.

The auditorium was darkened and became silent as Angela took her place on the podium and put up her first data slide. She took a sip of water, cleared her throat, and began speaking.

"In our study of adult male and female rats given a daily dose of OX312, we found the following: A ninety-two percent reduction in polygamous sexual encounters in comparison with baseline. The females postured for intercourse even though they weren't in estrus, but only with a single male. Similarly, males taking OX312 chose only one female partner. We subsequently performed functional MRI scans on the females and males and found that after taking OX312, region forty-three in the amygdala had reduced activity. This finding was significant to a P value of .01 versus our controls. Our MRI results correspond to similar findings in humans when we scan individuals deeply in love.

"In conclusion, on the basis of these results, we suggest that OX312 acts as a potential love potion in rodents. Further investigation of its use in human trials appears warranted."

There was polite applause from the audience. Then the moderator of the session asked, "Are there any questions for Dr. Chen?"

A man in the packed auditorium stood and walked to a microphone in the aisle. "Is the effect of OX312 direct on region forty-three or due to action in another part of the brain that consequently influences region forty-three?"

"Thank you for that excellent question," Angela said. "We used radio-labeled OX312, which is a derivative of the peptide hormone oxytocin. In animals that were subsequently sacrificed after administration, we found the radio-labeled drug strictly in area forty-three. Therefore we conclude the drug works by direct binding action on receptors located in that region of the brain. We are currently performing additional studies to specify which cellular receptor is affected."

The man at the microphone half-jokingly commented, "Are you suggesting the brain has a 'love receptor'?"

"Well, I think the implication is that suppressed activity in a focal region of the amygdala leads to behaviors associated with love, such as monogamous sexuality. We are presently in the early phase of our human study to assess if OX312 produces the emotional response and behavior associated with love."

"Any other questions for Dr. Chen?" the moderator asked. Someone new appeared at the microphone.

"Dr. Chen, were there any side effects of the drug?" The man spoke with an obvious British accent.

"Thank you for asking. No serious side effects have been experienced in over two years we have been working with the drug."

"Thank you," Paul Holfield said, returning to his seat.

"Unfortunately, our time is now up, and we must proceed with the next presentation," the moderator said. "Thank you, Dr. Chen, for sharing your intriguing findings. We look forward to hearing more about your work with OX312 in the future."

After she left the podium, Angela found herself surrounded by a group of eager questioners. While she tried to address inquiries the best she could, the next presentation was about to begin, so she excused herself and took a seat. When the last presentation of the session finished, Angela got up to leave. On her way out the auditorium door, she heard a voice from behind.

"Dr. Chen, if you have a moment?"

She turned around.

It was the man with the British accent who had asked her the question about side effects. "My name is Paul Holfield. May I tell you I was very impressed by your presentation?"

"Oh, thank you very much."

"Dr. Chen, I don't know if you've ever heard of Novara, the company I work for?"

"Of course I have. It's one of the largest pharmaceutical houses in the world."

"To be honest, I flew to New Haven on my way back to Switzerland just to hear your talk. If you have the time, I would like you to be my guest for dinner tonight."

"Well, the conference goes until six o'clock."

"I can send my driver to pick you up at your hotel at seven, if that works."

"That would be very nice. Yes, that sounds fine."

"All right then, I'll see you later."

As Holfield left, Angela headed in the opposite direction to attend a lecture she wanted to hear. On her way she thought, *Dinner on Novara. Wow! Someone out there is really interested in my work. How exciting.*

17

Vanessa followed Dr. Schaeffer as he visited with patients, going from one exam room to another in the outpatient clinic. She listened intently to his interviews and took copious notes. Her radiant beauty added something extra to the usually drab psych clinic ambiance.

Finishing the computer entry on his last patient of the day, Gabe turned to his visiting graduate student and said, "Well, I hope things today were interesting enough, even though violent criminal behavior wasn't on the menu with my patients today."

"Please don't view me as that narrow. I'm interested in a lot of other things besides violence. To the contrary, I found it fascinating how quickly you were able to get your patients expressing their innermost feelings. I don't know if I'll ever have the skill to do that."

"Thank you, but I'm certain that someday you will. However, it's not only the talking we do, but it's the medications as well which help make the difference. Everybody's brain has its own unique neurochemistry, and sometimes one drug works well for one person but not for someone else. I have found that with proper meds and counseling, most people with serious psychiatric illness can be restored to full functionality."

"That must give you a very satisfying feeling, helping so many people with disabling problems back to normalcy."

The clinic nurse was leaving and said, "I'll be off now, Dr. Schaeffer, see you back tomorrow. Will you close up?"

"I will, and thanks for all your help."

Gabe turned to Vanessa. "Have any plans for this evening?"

"No, I was just going to grab a quick dinner in the cafeteria and hit the library afterward."

"Would you like to join me for dinner?"

"Sure, that'd be nice," she said without hesitation.

"Do you like sushi?"

"I love sushi."

"There's a great place walking distance from the hospital. What if we go there?"

"That would be wonderful."

Gabe turned the lights off and locked the door as they left the ambulatory clinic. After arriving at the restaurant, they first ordered some green tea. Gabe poured each of them a cup, then raised his in a toast, saying, "To a good rotation."

"I'll second that," Vanessa said, smiling.

When the tray of assorted sushi arrived, Gabe asked, "How about some sake with the meal?"

"Sure, I'll give some sake a try."

Gabe ordered, and the server delivered a generous carafe to the table. The warm sake quickly took effect. As dinner continued they were talking and laughing like two old friends.

Turning personal, Vanessa said, "Hope you don't mind my asking but I'm curious. What made you go into psychiatry?" She already knew the answer from reading his file.

"It had a lot to do with my older brother Kirk. Growing up he was all anybody could ask for in a sibling. I was the bookworm, and he was the athlete, a star at any sport he tried. He was my best buddy. Kirk often hung out with me even though he could have been with his friends, and helped me in sports even though I was kind of a klutz. Then something strange happened in his junior year in high school. I can still remember it like yesterday. Kirk came home from school one day and wouldn't come out of his room. He said he wasn't feeling good. Then he didn't go to school the next day and didn't even leave his room to eat. When Kirk finally appeared, he didn't look like the brother I knew. His hair was disheveled, and he looked like he hadn't changed his clothes in days. When I tried to talk with him, he just didn't answer.

"My parents were at a total loss. They had no idea what to do. I was just plain scared. I didn't understand. One day Kirk took an overdose of Tylenol and ended up in the hospital with liver failure. A few weeks later, he died. I was devastated seeing him sick like that and be unable to do anything about it. It turns out there was a history of depression on my mother's side of the family. Kirk just was unlucky enough to get the depression gene along with all his good athletic ones. When I got older, I decided I wanted to do something to help other people like him who had serious psychiatric issues. Sadly, there's no way to go back in time and help Kirk, but nowadays, with proper medication, there is little doubt he would have been able to go on and lead a good life." Gabe sighed.

"I'm so sorry about your brother." Vanessa said reaching out to gently touch his hand in sympathy.

"What about you?" Gabe asked. "How did you end up in psychology?"

"It was nothing that complicated. I took psych in college, and it got me interested. After graduating I took a part-time counseling job and really liked it. Analyzing problems and figuring out how to help people in emotional turmoil, I really enjoyed that. I hope to finish formulating my master's thesis after this rotation, then who knows? Clinical practice, teaching, or both, I haven't made that decision yet."

"What kind of work have you been doing at Walter Reed?"

"I've been dealing with veterans suffering from post-traumatic stress. Mainly I do counseling for those with emotional scars left over from the battlefield. There is nothing that gives me pleasure more than seeing one of my vets leave a session able to smile again. That makes it all worthwhile."

"I hear you," Gabe said.

They ended the evening, each heading off on their own, but Gabe had a hard time getting Vanessa off his mind. He was whistling and had an unusually energetic bounce to his stride. *That woman has it all,* he thought, *brains, beauty, and sensitivity.* Gabe didn't realize it yet, but he was starting to fall in love.

18

Holfield's limo picked Angela up for dinner. The driver took her to the restaurant where her host and a companion were already waiting at the table.

"Ah, Dr. Chen, how good of you to join us tonight," Holfield said with a welcoming smile as he rose from his seat to greet her.

"Let me introduce you. This is Inger, a dear friend, and my administrative assistant at Novara."

"I've heard such good things about you from Paul," Inger said, then went on. "He believes you are doing groundbreaking research."

"Thank you." Angela said, blushing.

"Well, tonight, Dr. Chen, I want you to relax and enjoy yourself," Holfield said. "After a stressful day of presenting research in front of an audience filled with distinguished scientific critics, a little downtime seems highly appropriate." Holfield hailed over a waiter, and asked. "Shall we have a bottle of champagne for our table?"

"That sound good to me," Inger answered.

"And for me too," Angela said.

Holfield turned to his guest. "As I mentioned to you earlier, I flew in to New Haven just to hear *your* talk."

"You did?" Angela said, surprised.

"Yes. My work for Novara involves searching for new products to enhance our company pipeline, and I just happened to come across an abstract of your presentation. Your research intrigued me."

The waiter appeared with the champagne, pouring each a glass. Paul took the first sip, then exclaimed, "Ahhh! Dom Perignon is the very best. Is it not?"

Angela tasted some of the effervescent golden liquid. She wasn't a connoisseur of champagnes, but knew she was drinking something very special.

"It's excellent," Angela told her host.

"Perhaps you may find this bit of history interesting. It was a Benedictine monk somewhere in France during the 1600s, doing research on making sparkling wine that came up with the magical formula we are drinking in our glasses tonight. It's a little like what you do, Angela, in your laboratory. The monk toiled hard at experimenting with new ideas in fermentation until one of his findings made it all worthwhile."

Holfield was correct in his odd analogy and gave Angela the feeling that he really understood her. She told him, a bit giddy from the alcohol, "I never thought of myself as a Benedictine monk, but I couldn't agree more with what you said."

The trio ate appetizers and then a main course. As dinner was coming to a close, Holfield changed the direction of their conversation. "Dr. Chen, do you remember I asked you about OX312's side effects after your presentation?"

"Yes, I do."

"The pharmaceutical house that I represent, Novara, has an unblemished record, as far as product recalls or lawsuits over complications are concerned. Our firm is very sensitive on that issue. Any new drug we spend many millions on bringing to market can become an even more costly financial disaster if it's found to cause problems once in general use. Perhaps it is a bit premature to ask, but what makes you so sure that even though your drug doesn't seem to bother rats, it wouldn't cause a serious complication in humans?"

Angela answered confidently, "Well, I can't be one hundred percent sure. However, may I share a confidential piece of information with you, off the record?"

"Why, of course you can. Please think of myself and Inger as friends. Tell us anything you like."

Angela looked at the two earnestly and told them, "Dr. Schaeffer and I have been studying OX312 in human subjects for some time. Our data is still provisional, so it's not ready for presentation. However, I am happy to report that so far, we have not had one significant complication."

Holfield's eyebrows rose. "You don't say?"

"And by the way, one of those persons who used the drug was me!"

"You took OX312 yourself?" Angela nodded back in confirmation. "Impressive," Holfield said, his eyes widening. "If *you* actually tried it, then you obviously have great faith in its safety."

"I do indeed," she said with confidence. Her lips loosened by the effect of alcohol, Angela went on. "And as far as love is concerned, based my own experience, I can tell you it works in humans just as it seems to in the animal studies. OX312 induces an extremely intense emotion of love and associated behaviors."

"I must say, that's quite remarkable."

"The formulation of OX312 took a lot of hard work to develop. It's based on the molecular structure of oxytocin. Initially, computer modeling suggested it would work to turn on aggressive, violent behavior by blocking the oxytocin receptor. However, our study in rodents and now in humans confirms showed just the opposite. It induces *love* instead."

"Where do you see this drug going from here?" Holfield asked.

"Well, I am currently using it for couples experiencing severe marital discord. If taking the drug improves emotional bonding, as appears to be the case so far, many marriages could be saved." Holfield listened intently as Angela went on. "Unfortunately, Dr.

Schaeffer and I recently lost the major funding source for our work. So things are on hold for now."

"Funding?" he asked again.

"Yes, our government grant was recently terminated. I guess we weren't high enough on their priority list in the face of budget cuts."

"Well, relying on the government, that's what always happens. They have little capacity for insight into revolutionary innovation, but they are very good at cutting grants. If my opinion matters, the important research you're doing cannot be allowed to wither away."

"I appreciate that, but right now my hopes rest with Dr. Schaeffer. He's been trying hard to find some new avenue of funding. Unfortunately, all we have left is enough emergency money to last until the end of next month."

This is going to be all too easy, Holfield thought. "Dr. Chen, what if I told you I could write you a check tonight that will cover the next two years of research, plus a generous stipend for you and Dr. Schaeffer? In that way your work could continue without interruption."

Angela couldn't believe her ears. "You mean…"

"Yes, Novara will give you all the financial support you need to complete your work on the study you just spoke about."

"That would be a miracle."

"Well, I'd like to help make that miracle happen." Holfield smiled broadly as he continued. "All I ask in return is that Novara has the rights to any commercial production of OX312, should your human studies prove successful."

Angela had a hard time speaking but eventually was able to get out, "I—I don't see why not."

"Wonderful. Then we have a deal!" Paul exclaimed.

"Yes, it's a deal."

The two shook hands, then Holfield reached in his jacket pocket and pulled out a checkbook. He wrote out a check

LOVE POTION: A MEDICAL THRILLER

and handed it to Angela. Her hand trembled as she took it. She stared at it in the dim restaurant light but could make out the numbers—a four with five zeroes following it. Four hundred thousand dollars! Angela was beside herself. She felt like screaming with joy but mustering her composure, said, "Dr. Holfield, this is unbelievable. I cannot thank you enough. You are too generous."

"All you need to do is submit a quarterly progress report. I will have our home office draft a formal document of agreement and send it FedEx tomorrow. It will be at your lab by the time you get back to Boston from this conference."

"Wonderful!" Angela exclaimed. Then with a serious look on her face, she added, "Oh, just one more thing. I'll need to get the approval of my associate, Dr. Schaeffer."

"Of course, we will have a signature spot included for him as well. If Dr. Schaeffer should have any particular questions, he's more than welcome to contact me. In fact, if both of you would like to visit the Novara offices in Bern, I would be more than happy to arrange that. It is as simple as a phone call, and I'll send our company jet to pick you up and whisk you off to Switzerland."

They all laughed. Then Holfield said, "And now, ladies, may I offer you some dessert?" They both nodded yes, and Holfield waved the waiter over.

19

Vanessa joined Gabe on a site visit to examine inmates taking the experimental medication at Springhill. In the car on the way to the prison there was time to talk. Gabe wanted to fill her in on what to expect.

"Vanessa, let me caution you, it's a tough bunch of guys they've got locked up in there," he told her. "While it's not a psychiatric facility, a fair number of the inmates have serious underlying mental disorders. They almost never see women walking around the facility, so don't be surprised by anything disturbing you see or hear. If it becomes unbearable, let me know. I'll take you to the visitors' lounge where you can hang out until I finish up."

"I'm sure I'll be fine," Vanessa reassured him. "Remember, I deal with vets at the Walter Reed clinic. I've already heard and seen all kinds of things, and managed to survive."

Gabe pulled his car into the parking area near the prison gate entrance. They exited and approached on foot. A metal door opened, allowing them inside, then shut behind them with a resounding clang.

The guard who greeted them inside said, "Hey, Doc, nice to see you again. It looks like you brought someone along this time."

"Yes, a colleague, Ms. Vanessa Trent. She's helping out with the research today."

"OK," the guard said. "You can both head on inside." He unlocked an additional security entrance, letting them progress into the building. Before he closed the door behind them, he said, "Doc, I hope she knows what to expect in there."

"Yes, I filled her in."

"Great. I hate it when someone goes in and then, only a few minutes later, has to get the hell out because it's just too wild for them inside."

"I entirely understand." Gabe told the guard.

"And so do I," Vanessa chimed in.

The final steel door slammed shut behind them. Gabe and Vanessa found themselves locked within the maximum-security section of the penitentiary.

There were no windows, just tiny slits in the walls located high up and out of reach that let in very little sun. Everything was lit by fluorescent lights. Walking down a long corridor, they came to another security door, where a camera mounted on the ceiling glared down at them. The door clicked open, letting them go inside.

Still there wasn't much evidence of human life. Prisoners were enclosed behind cells that had solid steel doors with small but thick glass windows permitting a look inside. All was silent except for the buzz of the fluorescent lights. A guard suddenly appeared from around a corner up ahead.

"Hey, Dr. Schaeffer. Good to have you back." It was Neal White, the chief of security, who spoke as he approached.

"Say, Neal, let me introduce you to Vanessa Trent, my research assistant this month."

"Nice to meet you," Neal said to Vanessa, his eyebrows rising when he saw how pretty she was.

As he walked alongside Gabe, the security chief whispered into his ear, "Wish I had someone who looked like her, working with me. But they probably wouldn't last the day in here."

The visitors were led through a maze of hallways to a room where one of Gabe's research subjects was quietly waiting.

"Your first subject, Frank Sylvester, is inside," Neal said. "And Doc, I really have to hand it to you. You're a miracle man as far as that guy goes."

"Come on, Neal, it's not me. It's the drug that's made the difference."

"Well, Frank was as savage a maniac as anyone I've ever seen. It used to take several of us just to walk him to and from the shower in shackles, and you never knew what to expect. The last time Frank had a cellmate, he nearly killed him. When I asked what the man did to deserve his beating, Frank told me 'the damn asshole used my toothpaste.' That sounds like a legitimate reason to beat someone to within an inch of losing his life, doesn't it?"

The guard went on. "Frank held our prison's record for getting the most Taser shocks. But, it's all changed once he started that pill of yours. He's been working in our kitchen regularly, and says he want to be a cook someday. Of course, it'll be another four years before he's up for parole, so he'll have plenty of time to perfect his culinary skills."

Neal unlocked the examination room door for Gabe and Vanessa to enter. "I'll be watching from the room on the other side of the one way mirror just in case of any problem."

"Thanks," Gabe said as he and Vanessa entered the examination room.

"Hi, Doc," the man said, standing and extending his hand to shake Gabe's.

"Nice to see you again, Frank. This is Ms. Trent, my assistant, who will be helping out today, if you don't mind."

"Sure, Doc, that's no problem," Frank said. "And I've got to say, you really know how to pick good-looking help."

"Thanks for the compliment, and good morning, Frank," Vanessa said back.

After taking their seats across from the prisoner, Gabe pulled a file out of his briefcase and handed it to Frank. Then he handed him some paper and a pencil.

"You mean I got to take another test?"

"Just a short one this time, it won't take but a few minutes."

"And I love those questions. What would you do if you saw a dog hit by another car lying in the road? A. Call for help, B. Run it over, C. Avoid striking the animal and continue on, D. Pick it up and take it to the nearest vet? You remember my answer, Doc?"

"Yes. You crossed all of them out and added your own, E. Shoot the damn dog and put it out of its misery."

"I can't believe I wrote that, Doc."

"You couldn't help it, Frank. I'm sure you wouldn't do that again now."

"I was plain nuts, Doc, before I started that pill of yours."

"Not nuts, Frank, you just had a chemical imbalance that was making it really hard for you to control your frustration and anger."

"Well, whatever it was, I can't thank you enough."

In a few minutes, Frank finished, then handed the paper over to Gabe.

"Thanks. Let me ask you a couple of questions, if I could."

"Sure, fire away."

"Have you had any physical ailments since the medication started? What about loss of appetite, stomachache, headache, or sore muscles?"

"No, Doc, nothing unusual at all."

"Are you experiencing any nightmares or strange thoughts?"

"No."

"Good," Gabe said. "Then we'll say good-bye today and plan to see you again in a month."

Gabe waved at the mirror, signaling he was through. Neal was sitting outside looking in, but by agreement had the sound turned off. A few moments later, the door to their room was unlocked and opened.

Everyone stood up as Frank prepared to leave. "Oh, Doc, here, take back your pencil." He handed it over to him. "A sharp pencil could be considered a weapon in here, and I don't want to get in any trouble."

"Thanks Frank. I forgot."

"And I hope to see again," he said, directly addressing Vanessa.

"Appreciate you allowing me to sit in," she told the inmate before he walked out.

They did five more interviews before leaving late that afternoon. Vanessa was impressed. The prisoners had histories of murder, aggravated rape, and other brutal violent crimes, yet when interviewed looked and sounded like normal people. There wasn't the hint of anger in their tones. It was remarkable. Of all the subjects were who were taking the OX312, none seemed like they belonged behind bars.

As Neal led the group down the corridor toward the prison exit, they passed an inmate mopping the floor. His legs were in irons, but his arms were free. He had a circle of swastikas tattooed around his neck and one in the middle of his forehead, along with a pile of skulls on one arm. Vanessa thought she detected a subtle sneer on his face when he glanced at them walking by. Then it happened so fast, there was no time to respond.

The man dropped his mop and stepped forward, grabbing Vanessa from behind. He clutched her by the throat with one hand. In the other, he held what looked like a toothbrush with a sharp metal spike tied at its tip, and pushed it against her neck.

The quickness of his move took Gabe and Neal completely by surprise.

"OK, asshole," the inmate said to Neal. "Unlock the leg-irons, or the bitch is dead."

Neal pulled his gun, but it was impossible to take a shot without hitting Vanessa.

"Put the fucking piece down," the inmate ordered. Neal hesitated to part with his weapon. The skinhead pressed the metal spike against Vanessa's jugular, indenting her skin. "Do it now!" He screamed.

Neal looked helplessly at Gabe. He had no choice. Slowly he laid his gun on the ground.

"Go ahead and kick it down the hallway."

As ordered, Neal kicked the weapon well beyond his reach.

"Unlock my leg-irons."

Neal slowly removed a key from the chain on his belt and started to step forward.

"Stay where you are asshole," the inmate ordered the guard. "Give your key to the guy with the lab coat and let him do it."

The guard looked at Gabe apologetically, then handed him his key.

The prisoner barked out his next order. "Now get down on your hands and knees and crawl over."

Gabe was trembling. He knew the prisoner, Harry Salvino. Gabe had evaluated him as part of the OX312 study, but Salvino was randomly assigned to the control group, so he was receiving the placebo and not the actual drug. Gabe also knew from his record that Salvino was in jail for a series of vicious sexual assaults. As ordered, he got down on all fours and crawled over, unlocking the leg-irons.

"That's better," the prisoner said once his ankle irons were off. Gabe looked up at Vanessa, who struck him as surprisingly calm for someone with a sharp lethal weapon pressing against her throat. While Gabe slowly moved back to where the guard was standing, Vanessa spoke for the first time.

"Can you please loosen up? You're choking me."

"Shut up, bitch. You're my ticket out of this shit hole."

"Take it easy, Harry," the guard said, making an attempt to talk sense into the man. "If you hurt the lady, you'll be in here for life."

"I'm already in here for life, you dumb fuck!" Then the crazed inmate ordered, "Now step aside and let us pass."

Before the man could move forward, his arm flew to the side with a snapping sound. His makeshift weapon fell to the ground, and the prisoner's arm flopped uselessly down at his side. Meanwhile, Vanessa spun around and punched the skin-head directly in the throat, sending him gasping to the floor.

As she rubbed her neck, Vanessa addressed the attacker struggling to catch his breath. "I said that you were choking me. Sorry, but you should have listened and loosened up."

Gabe and the guard were aghast. They looked at each other in disbelief. Then Neal ran over, pressing an alarm button on the opposite wall. He bent down to handcuff the prisoner, who screamed in pain when his broken arm was moved. A moment later the hall was filled with other guards. However, the inmate was no longer in a fighting mood.

"I need a doctor!" the man called out. "My arm is killing me!"

"His arm will need a cast," Vanessa said. "I'm sure it's broken."

The guard looked at Vanessa in amazement and exclaimed. "Holy shit! Where did you learn how to do that?"

Vanessa wasn't going to tell them she had years of practice in martial arts as part of her CIA operational requirements. "Oh, it's just part of our training routine at Walter Reed. Before we were allowed to work on the closed psych ward, everyone has to take a course in self-defense."

"I guess you must have been the best in your class," Neal quipped. "You just made Bruce Lee look like a rookie. Anytime you like, you have an open invitation from me to come back and help train my staff."

On their ride back to Boston, Gabe kept thinking about the incident. He felt guilty about inviting Vanessa along and expos-ing her to the risk of being inside the high-security prison. He figured she was still a little shell-shocked from the episode and hoped she wouldn't suffer any post-traumatic symptoms.

"Vanessa, I'm really sorry about having you come along today," Gabe said remorsefully.

"This wasn't your fault. Even if I had to go back tomorrow, it really wouldn't bother me."

"I'm glad to hear you say that now, but you might not feel that way by tomorrow. You know as well as I do that a traumatic event might start bothering you days from now. Will you at least let me work my own guilt off by inviting you over to my place for dinner? I can do some incredible things with a wok. And please don't call me Dr. Schaeffer anymore. Gabe is just fine."

"OK, Gabe. That's an offer I can't refuse."

"Will eight p.m. work for you?"

"That sounds fine. Shall I bring anything with?"

"No thanks. Just bring yourself."

Gabe was silent for the balance of the ride back, but inside he was ecstatic Vanessa took his invitation. He was going to cook up something very special.

20

Vanessa went home to prepare for dinner at Gabe's. After entering her apartment, she used the secure phone to call Mueller.

"This mission is going to be a lot easier than I thought," she told her boss. "Schaeffer has invited me over for dinner tonight."

"I didn't say it was going to be difficult. It just required your particular talent set."

"I'll take that as a compliment. Anyway, Schaeffer's OX312 is some kind of drug."

"What do you mean?" Mueller asked.

"It really does turn violent criminals into pussycats. I saw it for myself. Schaeffer took me along to the maximum-security prison at Springhill where he does clinical research on the inmates. I can assure you that on treatment they are better behaved than either you or I."

"What do you mean by that?" Mueller quipped. "I'm the consummate gentleman."

"Sure. Like when you had me on mission in Caracas. If I remember correctly, you told me to, and I quote, 'Make it hurt bad, really bad, but don't quite kill him so he will never forget.'" She paused, then laughed. "Yes, I agree. You are some gentleman."

"Look, I am a nice guy to friends of the United States, but not to its enemies."

"I'll give you that. Anyway, from what I saw at Springhill, Schaeffer's drug might be just the thing to use on terrorists. If it can turn a serial killer into someone who won't step on an ant, I wouldn't be a bit surprised if jihadists on the medication tell us what they know just by asking nicely."

Mueller thought for a moment. "Why don't you get hold of some OX312 and send it to me? I'll see to it that the PSYOPs people get it. Then we'll find out if the stuff is really all that it's cracked up to be."

"That shouldn't be too hard. Give me a couple more days, and I'll have Schaffer doing whatever I want." She looked at the time, then exclaimed, "Oh shit! I'm meeting him for dinner in less than an hour. I've got to get my ass in gear."

"OK, go doll yourself up, and *bon appétit.*"

***

When Gabe heard his doorbell ring, he made a final mad rush to hide as much of the clutter around his apartment as possible. His heart was pounding, and his palms were a little sweaty as he opened the door to greet his guest.

"Wow!" Gabe exclaimed, dazzled by the transformation that had taken place in Vanessa since earlier. "Sorry. It's just you—you look so different."

"Well, I hope it's for the better."

"Yes, you look lovely."

Vanessa wore a form-fitting red cocktail dress with a plunging neckline and high heels. She was stunning to behold.

"Oh, come on in," Gabe said, after standing goo-goo eyed at the door's threshold, he had momentarily forgotten let her inside.

Entering his apartment on the seventeenth floor, Vanessa had an immediate look out the condo's floor-to-ceiling picture windows. "Gabe, you have an incredible view of Boston Harbor."

"I like it here on the waterfront. When I have time and weather permits, which unfortunately isn't too often, I try to go sailing." He walked over to the window next to where Vanessa now stood. "Let me show you something."

Gabe pointed to a spot far below. "If you look over there, you can make out my boat. It's the red twenty-eight footer in between those two big yachts."

"Yeah, I see it."

"Sailing is my passion. Bought the boat used, but it handles like a charm. There's nothing I love more than feeling the wind and sea spray whip by when I'm on the ocean." He paused for a moment, then continued. "We will have to make some arrangements for you to go sail with me. I think you'd really enjoy it."

"I bet I would. I'm originally from landlocked Nebraska. I've never been on a sailboat before."

"Then for sure you will be in for a treat. Now, can I offer you a glass of wine?"

"Definitely," Vanessa said.

"Do you prefer red or white?"

"It doesn't matter. Whatever you have is fine."

Gabe opened the bottle of Pinot Noir and poured his guest a glass. "Let's sit down and have something to eat. Hope you brought a good appetite because I made this dish I call Shanghai goulash. There's probably enough to feed four."

They ate by candlelight, and as darkness fell across the harbor, the moonlight shimmered off the water below. They were on their second bottle of wine, and had moved over to the sofa in his living room.

Gabe was in heaven. Vanessa made him feel perfectly at ease. She even giggled at his corny jokes.

"You know, I won the Boston to Provincetown regatta several years back."

"That's pretty impressive."

"It wasn't that tough," Gabe bragged. "When you're the big shot attending at Boston General, you find the strongest medical students on your clinical service, take them out for one or two sailing lessons, and like magic you win. At least it's the formula that worked for me."

"I guess there are some unforeseen benefits of being chief of service." Vanessa was in stitches over his confessed racing strategy, and Gabe was laughing at himself just as hard.

"Here, take a look at this." Gabe picked up a sailing magazine from the coffee table by the sofa. He thumbed through the pages until he reached the one he was looking for.

"This," Gabe said, pointing to the picture of a forty-five-footer, "is what I want. I've had my eye on this baby for a while. If I ever win the lottery, this is the boat I'd get."

Vanessa bent over to take a closer look. Gabe had a good view of her body's contour only inches away. He felt himself getting aroused.

"That's a gorgeous boat," Vanessa said, then added, "I hope your dream comes true."

Sitting on the sofa, with inhibitions lowered by wine, Gabe reached over and pulled her close. When their lips met, she willingly opened up to him. He began to undo the back of her dress, and there was no objection. She seemed to want him as much as he wanted her. In another minute they were naked. Gabe caressed her breasts and ran his hand up her thigh to the moist softness between her legs. She yielded to his touch, then pulled him down on top, moaning in ecstasy as he entered her.

For the time being, sailboats and his profession were forgotten. The neurochemistry taking place inside Gabe's brain was entirely consistent with falling in love.

21

Gabe awoke to find himself alone in his bed. He rubbed his eyes hoping that what he remembered of the night before had really happened. Suddenly, Vanessa popped her head through the bedroom door and said, "Come on, sleepyhead, breakfast is waiting."

"I'll be a minute," Gabe said, jumping out of bed and throwing on some shorts. Vanessa was out on the balcony. He joined her at the table, where she had their meal ready.

It was Saturday morning, and Gabe was not on call, so he was perfectly free to do as he wished.

"Last night was incredible," he said.

"Yes, it was," she said, smiling back and looking deeply into his eyes.

He took a sip of his coffee. "Say, if you don't have any plans today…"

"No, nothing special."

"We could sail to Marblehead if you like."

"Where's that?"

"Just a couple hours up the North Shore coast. We can eat an early dinner up there. I guarantee you'll love it."

Vanessa was silent for a moment, pretending to contemplate her options, then answered. "Sure, let's do it."

"Fantastic!" Gabe joyfully exclaimed. He wanted very much to share something special, like his sailing, with the woman he found so irresistible.

"Why don't I go home and pick up a few things after we finish breakfast? It won't take long."

"Fine," Gabe said, then added, "And please bring along something warm to cover up with. It gets cooler out there on the water than you might think, especially when the sun starts to go down."

Vanessa took a last sip of coffee, got up from the table she had cleaned up, and kissed Gabe good-bye. Just before the door to his apartment closed, she turned back, then said, "I'll be back before you could set a jib."

As the door to his apartment shut, Gabe thought, *Set a jib, huh? How did she know about a jib if she was never on a sailboat?*

22

Angela marched triumphantly into Gabe's office at the hospital early Monday morning.

"So, did you enjoy the meeting in New Haven?" he asked.

"It was very interesting," she answered nonchalantly.

"That's all you have to say for your week in Connecticut? How did the audience react to your presentation on OX312?"

Angela was so excited, she thought she might burst, but tried hard not to let on.

"Oh, it was OK. There were a few good questions afterward."

"That's nice. I sure wish I could have been there with you."

"I'm sorry you couldn't come," Angela said with sadness in her voice. "Any luck with our money situation while I was away?"

In truth, with Angela gone and Vanessa occupying much of his time, Gabe hadn't devoted any real effort to securing a new funding source for their research.

"Well, I don't have anything definite to report as yet. We still have a few weeks left before our emergency account runs dry. Hopefully, something will materialize between now and then."

"That's a shame," Angela told him, still keeping her good news under wraps. "Oh, here, there's something I want to show you. I brought this souvenir back from New Haven." She unceremoniously opened her purse, took out Holfield's check, and handed it to him.

"What's this?" Gabe asked, taking the check from her and looking it over. His eyes suddenly widened. He looked up at Angela in sheer disbelief.

"This can't be true. It's made out to our research fund for four hundred thousand dollars!"

"It's true, all right," she said, the excitement building in her voice. "We don't have to worry any longer. The money is for us to continue working with OX312!"

Angela put her arms around his neck and kissed him. "This is incredible. Where did it come from?" Gabe was mystified. Angela still had her arms around him.

"It came from the man whose signature is at the bottom, Paul Holfield. He's a bigwig at Novara Pharmaceutical in Switzerland. Holfield told me he was doing business stateside and decided to attend the New Haven conference just to hear my research abstract presented. Afterward he invited me out to dinner, and I told him more about our work using OX312."

"I guess Holfield was pretty impressed, based on the number he wrote out on this check." Gabe had a hard time getting his head around the story Angela told him. "What's the catch?"

"I'm sorry. What do you mean?" she shot back.

"Angela, nobody is going to plunk down this kind of cash without expecting something major in return."

"There's no catch," she said defensively. "Well, just a few provisos. For one, we have to send quarterly updates on the clinical studies, and we also have to give Novara exclusive rights to commercial production if the human research has positive results."

Like a parent to a child, Gabe said, "Oh, you promised them exclusive rights, did you? I'm not so sure—"

"But, Gabe, think about it. Holfield said he would not interfere in any way with how we choose to do our work. Let's face it, if the data proves positive, then we should want to see the drug made in quantity for clinical use. We certainly can't mass produce it in our small research lab. What could be better than having a world-class pharmaceutical company willing to get on board and help?"

Gabe thought for a moment. "I have to admit, what you're saying makes good sense."

"Then let's take the offer. You won't have to go groveling to everyone on the planet looking for additional funding. We have all we need right here in the check you're holding and then some. Please, Gabe, just say yes, and I'll go deposit it in our research account this afternoon. We should be receiving some documents from Novara by FedEx by later today. All we have to do is sign them, and the deal will be sealed."

He hesitated for a moment, still reluctant about signing away their rights, but finally acquiesced. "OK, what the hell? Let's go ahead and do it."

"Fabulous!" Angela exclaimed, jumping up and down like an excited little girl.

Vanessa happened to walk in on the celebration. "Oh, please excuse me. I didn't know—"

Gabe quickly turned from Angela toward Vanessa and called to her as she was about to walk out of the office. "Vanessa, it's OK. Come on back. You're not disturbing us. This is someone I want you to meet."

Angela immediately noticed the difference in Gabe's demeanor. She couldn't quite put her finger on it, but his mood totally changed. He jumped up from the seat at his desk, and excitedly walked over to the new arrival.

Gabe was smiling from ear to ear when he turned to Angela and told her, "This is Vanessa Trent. She is rotating with me on the clinical service this month. Vanessa is from the Walter Reed program and started on the clinical service last week while you were away. I'm sure you'll do everything you can to help make her experience at here as productive as possible."

It was obvious to Angela that in less than one minute, Gabe seemed to have forgotten about her, the projects, and the important check she had just shown him. Angela tried but couldn't produce a genuine smile for his guest. As she looked at Gabe, and the pretty blonde woman at his side, a completely unsettling thought entered her mind. *He's acting like a man in love.*

Angela stood speechless for a moment, then finally said, "Why, of course. I'll do everything I can. If you want to visit the lab, just give me a holler, and I'll be happy to do a tour."

Perhaps it was unjustified paranoia, but Angela now felt like the intruder. Uncomfortable in their presence, she excused herself.

"I've got to head off to the research building to finish setting up an experiment. Nice meeting you, Ms. Trent."

Angela quickly brushed by Gabe and Vanessa, who seemed oblivious to her departure.

After she went to the research building, and closed the lab door behind her, she sat at her desk and began to sob.

"How could he?" she plaintively asked an empty room as tears streamed down her face.

Angela didn't want to believe it, but the brutal truth couldn't be denied. Gabe Schaeffer, the man with whom she had collaborated for the last three years using a drug she had developed, the man whom she adored and had slept with only a short time ago, was in love with another woman.

23

Wearing a white lab coat, her blond hair pulled back, and black rimmed glasses, Vanessa looked every bit the psychotherapist. She could easily have passed for one of the full-time staff at Boston General's outpatient clinic.

Shadowing Gabe Schaeffer as he went from one patient to the next, Vanessa marveled at his clinical skills. He had an easy manner that permitted him to make an immediate connection to others. His treatment sessions weren't what she expected, with the patient divulging deep secrets from their childhood. Instead, Gabe probed about daily activities and how his patients reacted to events on an emotional basis.

Vanessa found him an intelligent sensitive man, and she thoroughly enjoyed his company. Her growing affection forced her to remember she was on an assignment that needed to be completed. The mission's goal wasn't frolicking under the bed sheets with Gabe Schaeffer. It was getting his OX312.

Before he finished seeing the last few patients of the afternoon, Vanessa asked, "Gabe, do you think I could stop by the research lab now? Afterward we could meet and go out for dinner."

"Sure," Gabe answered. "That sounds like a good idea. Angela should be there now. I'm certain she would be happy to show you around and tell you more about what she's doing in her experiments." Gabe looked down at his watch. "I'll be tied up about another hour or so finishing up with patients and charting."

"I wonder if you're as nice to all your visitors as you are to me," Vanessa whispered into his ear with a sexy voice. Glancing around and seeing that they were alone, she surprised Gabe with a kiss on the lips.

"Hey, watch out with that. If someone sees us—"

"No one saw, don't worry. That little kiss was within professional guidelines."

Gabe couldn't help himself. He grabbed Vanessa tightly, and kissed her passionately, allowing their tongues time to linger in play. Separating after the embrace, Gabe said, "Now that's from one professional guideline to another." They laughed as she headed toward the door.

"You're looking for room 306 in the research building," he said. "And good luck finding it. The halls over there are like a maze, complete with occasional dead ends. If you get lost, call me on my cell."

"Don't fret, I'll find it." Vanessa already knew the lab's room number and its precise location from information included in Schaeffer's file. She also knew all about Gabe's work associate, Angela Chen.

The file on Angela indicated her parents left the Chinese mainland and immigrated to California when she was an infant. Her father, Hue Chen, earned a PhD in mathematics, then taught at Berkley. Her mother eventually became a pediatrician. Hue Chen had a serious drinking problem, which had led to repeated episodes of domestic confrontation. Both parents were now deceased, and Angela had no siblings. She was a career scientist who received her PhDs in neurobiology and psychology at Harvard.

There was nothing about a physical relationship between Schaeffer and Chen included in the agency file, but Vanessa couldn't forget the icy glare Chen had given her when they first met. It made her wonder whether the research assistant had feelings for her colleague that went beyond their research.

Regardless, Vanessa wanted things to be smooth between them. Having someone like Chen around with ruffled feathers wouldn't do her mission any good. So when she went to visit with her at the lab, Vanessa intended to make nice.

She stood outside room 306 in the Boston General Research building and knocked on the door.

"Hold on, I'll just be a minute," Angela responded, as she was administering a dose of OX312 to one of her experimental rats. When she finished, Angela took off her protective gloves and goggles, then went to the door. Ever since she was attacked by a stranger who snuck into the lab, Angela made sure the door was always locked. At her request, building security installed an additional deadbolt, and just in case, she now kept a Taser tucked away in her desk.

"Who's there?" Angela asked.

"It's Vanessa."

She opened the door. "Oh, hello," Angela said halfheartedly.

"I wanted to take you up on your offer to visit the lab, and see firsthand the work you're doing."

"Well, come on in." Angela said, moving aside and permitting Vanessa to enter. "I can assure you there's nothing that mysterious going on in here, just nuts-and-bolts neurobiological research." The room Vanessa entered was an office with a sofa, two desks, and computers.

"We share a pretty generic office." Angela pointed. "That desk over there is mine, and this one is Dr. Schaeffer's. We do our data analysis and paperwork in here."

Angela led Vanessa from the office into an adjacent large, brightly lit laboratory with all the things Vanessa expected to see: sophisticated-looking glass tubing, centrifuges, and a metric scale. Angela walked over to a small operating table at the room's center.

"Unfortunately, the worst part of the research is that I must sacrifice some of the animals in order to analyze their tissues."

Angela held up a glass container filled with liquid that had a tiny walnut shaped structure floating inside. "After removal, the brain is run through a series of tests looking for the precise anatomic regions where OX312 administered is located."

"How very interesting," Vanessa said, nodding her head in acknowledgment.

From there Angela took her visitor to another room. Before they entered, Angela said, "You need to leave anything with iron in it out here. Otherwise it could get sucked into the strong MRI magnet."

Vanessa took a cell phone out of her lab coat pocket and left it on the consul outside. Inside the room was a sophisticated looking piece of medical equipment that emanated a low pitched humming sound.

"This is the special scanner we use to run our animal subjects through, looking for changes in brain metabolic activity. It's smaller than a typical whole-body MRI because it's just meant for the head size of our experimental animals. Human subjects we study get scanned on the larger and more powerful MRI over at the hospital."

Angela led Vanessa into another room, one filled with dozens of caged rats. "Here are our subjects. Would you like to hold one?"

"No, that's quite all right," Vanessa answered.

"Let me show you something else you might find interesting." Angela brought Vanessa over to the computer screen at the back of the room, and brought up some images. "These are enlarged MRI slices through the brain of one of our rats. On the left you see the image before treatment with OX312, and on the right, after."

The striking differences were obvious even to Vanessa.

"The color-coded areas represent metabolic activity in the brain," Angela said, pointing out the important findings. "The red color indicates high metabolic activity in an area associated with aggressive behavior. After treatment the scan shows blue in the same place, indicating that activity has slowed. The aggressive rats that would snarl and bite at the slightest provocation become as peaceful as field mice when OX312 is administered. You don't even need protective gear like gloves or goggles to handle them once they receive the medication."

"What about this area over here that turned red after treatment?

"Interesting you should notice that. It's not a large region, but it's a pretty important one. That location is the current focal point of my work. It is activated when rats are sexually active, and OX312 causes it to turn on like a light bulb. If you're wondering about humans, we've seen the same effect in those people we've studied."

"You mean you've discovered the brain's G-spot?"

"Well, that might be one way of looking at it," Angela said, blushing. "But it's more complex than just sexual activity, even in rats. They become monogamous when that area lights up and behave as if they've fallen in love with one partner."

"Do you administer the OX312 by injection?"

"No, it's given orally." She walked over to the other side of the room, to a safe with an alphanumeric lock on the front. Vanessa watched her plug in the numbers 603, the opposite of the room number, and the door clicked open. Inside Vanessa could see a container filled with small yellow tablets and several vials containing a yellow powder. Angela reached inside and pulled out one of the vials filled with a yellow substance.

"This is OX312," she proudly announced. Angela handed the vial over to Vanessa. "We measure out the amount we need based on weight and feed it to the experimental animals."

"What are the tablets for?"

"Oh, those pills are for our human subjects. Dr. Schaeffer is working with violent inmates at Springhill penitentiary. We compound the powder into tablet form using that machine over there." Angela pointed to a pill press located under a lab hood at the far side of the laboratory. "I've been using the medication in a couples study, looking at the effects on those experiencing severe marital discord."

Vanessa held up the vial of yellow, powdered OX312. "So this is what all the excitement is about, your *love potion*."

"Yes, and rightfully so. While Dr. Schaeffer believes OX312 can curb explosive violent behavior, my hope is that one day the drug will make a big difference for marriages teetering on the brink of collapse. "

"How much of this do you feed the rats?"

"Only one-tenth of a gram daily does the job."

"How much would a human subject need?"

"We use a one-gram tablet for an average-sized human subject of either sex. Here, let me show you something else." Angela took back the vial and put it back in the safe.

They walked over to another door, which she cautiously opened, and both went inside. The lights were low but on. A large, square table covered by a clear glass dome sat inside. Vanessa could see the rat inhabitants scurrying about their enclosed territory.

"This is our rodent city," Angela said. "Inside the ambient conditions of lighting, noise, and feeding times are controlled. As the population density increases to a critical level, the behavior of the rats begins to change. The males become uniformly aggressive and fight nearly continuously. The sexual behavior becomes aberrant, with strange things happening, like the males trying to have intercourse with other males. The behavior of the females is also altered. They refuse sexual encounters with the males even during estrus and sometimes are severely injured when doing so. We find an occasional mother eating one of her offspring. Thing become so wild in there, Gabe nicknamed it *Dodge City*, like the old Wild West."

"But," Vanessa said, "everything inside looks so peaceful."

"Yes, for now because they're getting fed a regular dose of OX312 daily. Give them forty-eight hours without the drug, and then it goes up for grabs in there."

"How intriguing this all is. Angela, I must say it looks like you are doing some brilliant research." Vanessa went on with the compliments. "You must be very proud of your work. Dr. Schaeffer certainly speaks very highly of your abilities."

Angela smiled for the first time since Vanessa arrived. "Thank you. That's kind of you to say." Angela glanced at her watch, then said, "I've got to start cleaning up and get ready to leave for the evening. I need to get some rat chow from the storeroom down the hall. If you can hang around, I won't be but a minute or two. Then I can walk you back to the hospital so you won't get lost in this crazy place."

This was opportunity handed to Vanessa on a silver platter. "Sure, I'll wait for you, and take your time. No way could I find my way back to the hospital on my own," she lied.

Angela left the office and locked the door from the outside. After Vanessa heard her footsteps fade away down the hall, she quickly went to the safe containing the OX312 and pressed in the combination, 603. The door clicked open. Vanessa took out one of the vials containing the yellow powder, put it in her purse, and relocked the refrigerator door by entering the code again. The entire process of pilfering the experimental drug took less than a minute. Vanessa hurried into the front office, picked up a magazine that lay on the desk, and started thumbing through the pages.

A few minutes passed, then Angela returned. "See, I told you I wouldn't be long." She carried a large bag filled with food pellets.

Vanessa smiled at her and thought, *But it was long enough for me to get what I needed.* "Would you like some help with the feeding?" Vanessa offered.

"Sure. It's easy to do, and we can get out of here quicker."

Afterward they walked out of the lab together. While Angela was leading her guest back to the hospital, Vanessa said, "Thanks again for sharing all that information with me."

"Don't mention it."

Vanessa felt like she had made some progress in establishing a cordial relationship with Schaeffer's possessive female colleague.

As they entered the hospital complex from the research building, Angela asked, "Any plans for this evening? Perhaps you'd like to join me for dinner?"

"Maybe some other time," Vanessa answered. "Unfortunately, I've got another obligation." The last thing she wanted to do was tell Angela those plans included dinner and sleeping with Gabe.

"Then good-night, Vanessa."

Each turned and headed off in an opposite direction. Vanessa had to move fast. She wanted to get home and freshen up before meeting up with Gabe for dinner at a place yet to be determined.

***

Vanessa had just accomplished an important part of her mission, getting her hands on some OX312. It was a bonus that she enjoyed being in the company of Gabe Schaeffer. He was a far cry from the corrupt diplomats, weapons merchants, or drug runners she was used to dealing with. There was something very special about him that attracted her. She had to admit that so far, Mueller's prediction was correct. The mission was more like a vacation than work.

When Vanessa entered her apartment, she went into her bathroom and took out a bag containing her makeup. Removing some of her paraphernalia, she came across a small cylinder of eye shadow. Vanessa unscrewed its top and shook its contents into the toilet bowl, then flushed. Next she took the vial of OX312 and carefully poured a small portion of its contents into the empty makeup container. She closed the top and put it back inside the bag. *Why not?* She thought. *I might find it useful on a future assignment.* After she freshened up and dressed for the evening out, Vanessa picked up her secure phone and called her contact, a man she knew only as Alex.

Fifteen minutes later a motorcycle pulled up in front of the building where she stayed. The cyclist wore a helmet, which he didn't remove. Instead, he walked up the steps to Vanessa's apartment entry and pressed the buzzer. She quickly came down and handed him an envelope.

"Alex, there's something inside Mueller wants ASAP." Her contact, still wearing his helmet with the visor down, took the envelope, put it inside his leather jacket, but said nothing. He zipped up, then turned and marched down the steps back to his motorcycle. Alex got on and headed directly for Logan International Airport. He would take the commuter fight to DC. Before the night was over, Alex would personally hand the envelope to Mueller at Langley.

Vanessa hurried back upstairs, got her backpack, threw in a teddy, a change of clothes, her toothbrush, then flew out the door. Gabe had sent her a text to meet him at Faneuil Hall for dinner. She hailed a cab and headed off, excited by the thought of their night together.

24

Once Mueller had the vial of OX312 in his hands, he made a call. It was to Mark Jeffers at Gitmo. Jeffers was the chief PSYOPs man stationed at the detention center. He supervised interrogations of the terrorist combatants held there and was responsible for developing individual strategies for psychologically breaking them down. Jeffers was also responsible for making sure they didn't die in the process, which was considerably less likely now with the banning of 'enhanced' interrogation techniques, like water-boarding.

"Mark," Mueller said, "I've got a special gift for you that should be arriving shortly."

"What is it? My birthday isn't for another three months. Wait, you're sending me a case of Samuel Adams. The shit they call beer down here tastes like piss."

"No. It's something better than that. What I'm sending will make your life a lot easier, and our country much safer."

"OK, but that sounds like a tall order. Fill me in before I die of suspense."

"It's a drug that we think will pacify the most recalcitrant assholes you have caged in down there. I'm sending you a sample to try out. Only one gram a day by mouth is all it takes. You can mix it in their food, and they won't even know they are taking it."

"Violence is easy for us to control," Jeffers said. "We just bind the arms and legs, put mitts over their hands, and a face mask on so they can't bite. Getting information out of someone who thinks he's going to be rewarded with seventy-two virgins once he dies for his cause, now that's a different story. Ever since water-boarding has been banned, it's next to impossible for us to get good intel from these bums. By the way, I'm sure you realize the Geneva Convention prohibits the use of psychoactive drugs to extract information."

"Of course, I know that. But there's a loophole here. You can justify use of the drug for treatment of inmate depression. Just get one of your doctors to write the orders, and see if it works the way it's supposed to during questioning. You can swing that?"

"Well, I'll be happy to try. Hell, I'm kind of depressed down here myself. Maybe I should take a taste."

"Stick with beer," Mueller said, then continued. "If this stuff works the way we think it will, I should at least be entitled to a steak dinner on your government charge card the next time you come to DC. Do we have a deal?"

"We sure do. You buy the beers, and I will buy the steaks."

"Shit. Then it's going to be a really expensive evening for me."

"I love you, Mueller, and that's the first time I ever said that to a man."

"Suck my dick, Jeffers."

Mueller got off the phone and propped his feet up on the desk. *If OX312 worked on the prisoners at Gitmo, it would certainly help put an end to the motherfucking terrorists around the world.* Just the thought of that put a smile on his face.

25

A stunning raven-haired vixen sat at the piano bar in the Bellagio nursing a dirty martini. Natalie had an hour to kill until the appointment with her next client. His name was Jim Owens, or at least that's what he told her over the phone, and he was interested in high-quality companionship. That request was shorthand for having great sex while you were away from the wife back home.

Owens told her he was in town for a business convention like most of the other men she had a working relationship with. He was a first timer with her, so she took care to go over the details and make sure he understood quite clearly the way things operated.

"No problem, I've got the money," he told her with his Southern accent. "Put me down for two hours."

"Say, Jim, I take credit cards if you prefer," Natalie told him. "You just need to show me proper ID."

"No, honey," he answered. "Let's keep it cash."

The $4,000 price tag didn't seem to bother him. *From Houston, probably oil money,* she thought after their conversation was over.

Putting her phone away, she noticed a man in a fine, tailored suit take a seat next to her at the bar. He looked distinguished, with a full head of slightly graying hair, an elegant silk tie, and gold cuff links. She spotted a Rolex on his wrist.

He pulled out a cigarette and pretended to look for a light. "Got a match?" he asked her.

"Better than that," Natalie said, handing him a silver torch lighter.

"Thanks," he said.

The bartender took the man's drink order.

He started sipping at his vodka tonic. "You know where a guy can find some entertainment around here?"

"I'm not sure I know what you mean. In Vegas you have to be a little more specific. There are all kinds of options."

"I mean I've got some time to kill and thought I might find some female company."

"Here I am," Natalie offered.

"No, I mean the kind of company you do in private. I have a suite upstairs."

"That depends," Natalie told him. She was well aware of her time constraints, and prided herself on a reputation of always being punctual, but making some impromptu money before her upcoming appointment didn't seem like a bad idea. *This guy has a $15,000 watch on his wrist and gold cufflinks. That's a good sign.* Opportunity had just dropped in her lap, so why not take it?

"I don't come cheap," Natalie told him.

"I didn't think so, but I'm sure I can afford you."

"Fifteen hundred for thirty minutes, and you can do anything you want. Fuck me, or I'll suck you, or both, it doesn't matter. Anything but anal, that's a big no, no."

"Sounds good to me," he said, reaching in his pocket to pull out a wad of money. Just as he did, another man in a suit sat on her other side. She ignored the newcomer, trying to give full attention to her new client as he counted out the bills to give her, but the new arrival rudely tapped her on the shoulder. She turned to him.

"Hey, sweetie pie, you know that what you are doing is against the law." He laid his Las Vegas police badge on the counter in front of her.

"Oh shit," she said.

Meanwhile her presumed John with the Rolex was smiling, and took another sip of his drink.

"You're fucked," the officer with the badge told her, "but this time not in the literal sense." Then he added with the Southern accent he used over the phone, and by the way, I'm Jim Owens."

"This is entrapment," she said. "It will never stick in court."

"Wanna bet?" asked the detective with the vodka tonic. He produced a miniature tape recorder from his other pocket.

"Oh, you two are just full of surprises, aren't you? Where does a lowly cop like you get the money for a Rolex?" She turned to Jim Owens. "Why don't you give me a number and I'll pay you off now so we can forget about this whole thing? Then you can get yourself a Rolex like your partner."

"You mean the ninety-five bucks I paid for this Chinese knock-off?" Owens's colleague held up his wrist and chortled.

"Come along with us," the officer ordered, "and don't make a scene."

They walked Natalie to the hotel's security office and sat her down. Owens started filling out paperwork, while the other searched her purse.

"Look what we have here." He held up a vial of white powder. "I'd guess about ten grams in here. That should be enough to put you away for five to ten."

"Fuck you. I can afford the best lawyer in Vegas. He'll get me off, you'll see."

"Even Jesus Christ couldn't get you off on this one. I'm afraid you're going to end up doing serious jail time."

The head of hotel security took her picture to log into their database and told her, "No matter what happens to you after the police take you away, the next time we find you anywhere on our property, we'll throw you out on the street. Understand?"

Natalie was beside herself. She wanted to scream, but it wouldn't do any good. She knew the mayor of Las Vegas had just made a campaign promise to crack down on prostitution. But she never expected to get caught. The solicitation charge was no big deal, but cocaine possession was another matter. She had a big problem, a really big problem. Natalie shuddered at the thought of doing time behind bars.

26

Angela was upset. Ever since Vanessa Trent arrived at Boston General, Gabe barely gave her the time of day. The woman from Walter Reed had completely monopolized him. What could she do?

Her rival had blond hair, long legs, and a great body. Everything a typical man longed for. She hated that someone with Gabe's background could be so quickly snared by the attractive female newcomer.

Angela had a legitimate claim to OX312. After all, she had used computer modeling and custom designed the drug to fit tightly into the brain's oxytocin receptor. It was supposed to block oxytocin effect and facilitate aggression but instead produced unexpected activation one hundred times more powerful than oxytocin itself. It was a wonderful discovery, but it was really hers and Gabe hadn't given her proper recognition. Instead, he chose to shack up with a woman who had just come on the scene, someone he barely knew, and do it right in front of her face. *What an ingrate,* she thought.

There was something about Vanessa that struck Angela as phony, but she couldn't precisely put her finger on it. She decided to do her own check up on Vanessa's credentials. What was wrong with doing a little private investigation?

Angela called Walter Reed Medical Center. She asked to speak with the chief of the psychology division.

"This is Angela Chen calling from Boston General. I work with Dr. Gabe Schaeffer. Vanessa Trent has been visiting our department. Because we have radioisotopes located in our research area, I was wondering if you could send me her radiation badge so we don't have any problems with our safety officer. He's a real stickler for protocol.

"Vanessa is one of our best graduate students," Dr. Heffner said. "I'll have my secretary FedEx the badge to Dr. Schaeffer's office. No worries, you'll have it by tomorrow. Please say hello from me if you see her. Tell Ms. Trent I hope she's enjoying herself and learning a lot. Please give a special thanks to Dr. Schaeffer from me for allowing her to rotate at Boston General."

"Of course I will," she told him, with no intention of carrying out her promise.

When Angela hung up the phone, her frustration boiled over. *Sure she's enjoying herself, screwing the brains out of someone I really cared about.*

In the midst of her fury, Angela had an idea. *I'll give Gabe his due. Then let's see how he feels about it.*

Angela needed to extricate herself from the painful position she found herself in. Continuing to face the woman who was having an open affair with the man she loved was simply intolerable. Angela decided on something drastic, something that would never have entered her mind before. She got on the phone and put a call through to Paul Holfield at his office in Switzerland. His administrative assistant, Inger Kroll, answered.

"Oh, Angela, it's so nice to hear your voice again. How's the work on the OX312 coming along?"

"Oh, great…yes, great. My human study is recruiting more couples with marital difficulty every day."

"That's very good. It seems like everything is going according to plan."

"Well, not exactly, but I need to discuss that with Dr. Holfield."

"Of course, I'll put you right through." As she was about to transfer the call, Inger said, "Angela, by the way, thank you for sending back the signed document giving Novara production rights to OX312 so promptly."

When Holfield came on the line Angela spoke first.

"I wonder if I could share something with you in strict confidence."

"Sure you can."

"To be quite frank, Mr. Holfield, lately I've been quite unhappy in my position here at Boston General. I would prefer not getting into all the details, but thought if there were an opportunity for me to work at Novara in Switzerland, I would take it."

"Well, we certainly can't have a talented researcher like you be unhappy. Having you with us over here would be wonderful! We can have a lab set up for you here in a matter of days." Holfield paused, then went on. "Just one more question. What about Dr. Schaeffer? Is he going to let you bring OX312 to Switzerland?"

"Well, he doesn't have much of a choice. I designed the drug and began using it in my experiments. Dr. Schaeffer only became interested in its use after he saw the effects on blunting aggression in my rodent model."

"Didn't you work in his lab?"

"Yes, and I gave him access to my drug for his research, but the intellectual rights, those belong to me alone." She spoke defiantly, then paused briefly before continuing. "However, I wouldn't feel right stopping him from doing his research using OX312. He should be able to continue using the drug if he wants to."

"I completely understand. Tell you what. I'll check this out with our legal department. If they say your claim could stand up in court, you can pack your bags and head to Bern. We'll be waiting with open arms, and I can guarantee that we have so many people over here getting divorced, it will be easy to recruit couples for your clinical study."

"Thanks so much."

"I'll get back to you as soon as I get an opinion from legal."

***

Holfield was pleased. It would be much easier to deal with Angela Chen in Bern than with both her and Schaeffer in Boston. With her working in Switzerland, he reasoned Novara might have a new blockbuster on the market in no time…a love potion pill that would sell for a high price. And with a drug like that, black market sales could end up soaring past those of the standard prescription medication. Holfield saw big dollar signs. It would be a financial windfall for him and his company. *If any man or woman could get someone they wanted to fall in love with them with the help of a little OX312, why not?*

As far as the legal department, their decision made no difference to him. Even if Schaeffer had some legitimate claim to ownership of the drug, once Holfield had Angela Chen working for him there, a small-time physician had no chance of standing up to the powerful company which he ran.

27

Gabe looked through the pile of mail Mary Ann had laid on his desk. He began opening, then tossing away the items in the trash until he came across something that looked important. It was an invitation from the American Society of Neuropsychiatry to give a lecture at an upcoming conference in Aspen, Colorado. His assignment would be to give a talk about new approaches to the understanding and treatment of pathologically violent behavior. All his expenses would be paid, and he would get a $1,500 honorarium to boot.

Years before, Gabe had vacationed in Aspen during the winter to try skiing. Aspen was a magical place to stay, a winter wonderland. However, he found skiing more of a struggle for survival than pleasure. That was one sport which would never usurp his sailing. The lecture offer presented Gabe with an opportunity to be in the mountains during summer, and that would be a completely different experience. He contemplated the invite. *A few days in the mountains during nice weather, all expenses paid. Now that's an offer I can't refuse. Vanessa would love it.*

There was something else. Gabe was planning on proposing marriage to her. What better place in the world to ask Vanessa to be his wife than on top of Aspen Mountain? Gabe would surprise her with his important question at twelve thousand feet, overlooking the panorama around them. It was a perfect plan.

He rushed over to the medical library where she was study-ing. Gabe approached her and excitedly asked, "When was the last time you were in the Rocky Mountains during the summer?"

"Never," she said. "That's an odd question."

"No, it's not odd at all. I've just been invited to give a lecture in Aspen and thought you might want to come along. What do you say?"

She thought quickly. "That sounds like fun. Of course I'll go."

"Fantastic!" Gabe exclaimed loudly enough for other people in the quiet library to turn their heads and scowl.

***

It was no secret around the department of psychiatry that Dr. Schaeffer had a serious thing for Ms. Trent. When his clinic nurse, Cindy, was lunching together with Mary Ann, Schaeffer's secretary, they had a conversation about their boss.

"I've never seen him happier. " Cindy said. "You can bet he's getting it on with that good-looking lady from Walter Reed."

"Well, a great guy like Dr. Schaeffer deserves a terrific girl-friend. At least from what I've seen, in addition to her good looks, she seems to be a nice person, and is definitely no airhead." Mary Ann said, sticking up her boss's new love interest.

"I have to admit they do make a nice couple, but…" Then Cindy put a frown on her face. "But I'm kind of depressed."

"Why is that?" Mary Ann asked.

"I've been waiting years for him to ask me out, and now the blonde gets him after a few weeks."

"But, Cindy, you're married."

"Of course I'm married. But that doesn't mean I wouldn't take my ring off for Dr. Schaeffer, at least for one night."

"Shame on you," Mary Ann shot back as they shared a good laugh.

***

Jeffers called Mueller. "How's the weather up north?" he asked.

"It's in the seventies, and the sun's shining. But you could find that out in a second on the Internet. What's up?"

"Here the temperature is ninety-five degrees in the shade, and the humidity is the same. Plus the fucking mosquitoes are the size of hellfire missiles." There was silence for a moment while Mueller heard his friend take the gulp of a drink over the phone. Jeffers sighed. "That case of Samuel Adams you sent me is almost gone."

"OK, I get the message. I'll send down another. Is that the reason you called?"

"No, this isn't about more Sam Adams, but another case would be greatly appreciated. I wanted to give you an update on what we found with the drug you sent us. The OX312 is a fucking godsend. My interrogators are clamoring for more. It's like someone waved a magic wand over the turban heads, and they became our best friends. They'll tell you anything you want to know. Anyway, it should be me sending you something rather than the other way around. What about a box of Cuban cigars?"

"That's contraband. You can't buy that on an American base."

"True. But don't forget I also work for the CIA. We can get anything I want."

"You're right on that. I can already taste those *Cubans.*"

"Well, get me some more of that OX312 shit and pronto. By the way, I have the lab at Langley working on a small amount of the substance. Hopefully, they will have the chemical formula worked out pretty soon. It won't too be long after that, and we might be able to make our own."

"That's great. In the meantime I have my best agent working on getting the drug away from the Boston General folks so the agency is the only one who has it. Say, what's this I hear about Gitmo closing down?"

"I'll be the last one to object, but that's the rumor, and it's been the rumor for years. Just thinking about never have to use bug repellant again makes me smile. I assure you I won't be sorry if it happens. And if they do close us down, we'll just move our operation somewhere else. Somebody has to interrogate these sons of bitches. Anywhere would be better than this."

As Jeffers got off the phone, he burped loudly, then went back to looking over interrogation transcripts.

Mueller had the confirmation he was hoping for. He had to get OX312 out of circulation, and as quickly as possible. It was way too valuable for anyone else in the world but the CIA to control.

28

olmes drove his boss, Ferguson, into downtown DC. They were meeting Mueller for dinner.

"Russ, make sure you get the biggest steak on the menu," Ferguson suggested to his attaché. "The bill is on the CIA. They owe me big-time."

The driver nodded his head. "I understand, sir. That's an order I will definitely enjoy carrying out."

Holmes had worked for Ferguson for the last three years and had nothing but adulation for his superior officer. He was totally loyal to the man whom he viewed as one of the most dedicated and intelligent officers he had come across during his fifteen-year career.

Holmes had never been a combat soldier like Ferguson, who had distinguished himself as a Special Forces officer in Afghanistan before taking a job at the Defense Department. At state functions when Ferguson was in full dress uniform, he sported a collection of medals and ribbons across his chest, testimony to his heroism during battle. Holmes loved his country just as much as Ferguson, but his talents were in logistics and organization rather than fighting.

Russell Holmes's life in the military wasn't an easy one. Being a gay man posed special challenges. Regardless of official policy, he chose to keep his sexual preference and activity secret. His colleagues at Defense had no idea of his true persuasion. Holmes detested sitting with them in bars, drinking booze while listening to their endless banter about female conquests. Pretending to be one of the boys, he made up his own tall tales of bodacious heterosexual activity, but it upset him to no end that his public social life was all an elaborate charade.

Holmes's father was a devout Evangelical who loved Jesus and the Bible more than life itself. Admitting he was gay to his dad was unthinkable. His mother was the only family member who knew the truth and promised never to divulge. Yet, Holmes longed to be loved and accepted by others for the person he truly was...a loyal servant of the US government who just happened to be gay.

***

Ferguson entered the restaurant, while Holmes parked the car. The maître d' led Ferguson to a table where Mueller was already seated, nursing his vodka tonic.

They greeted each other with a special handshake, tightly grasping each other's right forearm. It was the way those who were members of the elite Special Forces said hello. They were brave men willing to risk their lives for their country and ask nothing in return.

"Good to see you, asshole," Mueller said to Ferguson, then went on.

"What took you so long? You're twenty minutes and one vodka tonic late. This is number two." Mueller tapped the nearly empty glass in front of him.

"What can I say? Holmes did the driving. He drives a little too defensively, if you know what I mean."

"You mean to say he drives like a freakin woman?"

"Well...yeah!" Both men laughed.

"He's parking the car and joining us tonight, OK?"

"Sure. It's fine by me as long as we are free to talk business in his presence."

"Say anything you like. He's got top security clearance, and I own his ass."

"Terrific," Mueller answered.

"Oh, don't forget dinner is on you."

"I knew that would be the first thing on your agenda, but I got good news for you. I'm treating for drinks also, so you can down scotches to your heart's content."

"Drinks as well, huh?" Ferguson said with a big smile on his face. "What is that about?"

"It's about the OX312. You were right. It turned out to be pretty good stuff."

Lieutenant Holmes joined up with them at the table. "You remember my attaché, Russell?" Ferguson asked.

Mueller shook hands with the new arrival, noting his wimpy grip, then answered, "Sure I do. How are you, Russ? Has your boss been treating you well?"

"Very well, thanks."

As the lieutenant took a seat, Mueller announced, "OK, guys, dinner and all you can drink on me." The effects of his vodka tonics produced a mild slurring to his speech. "If you guys want to order the thirty-six-ounce T-bone, be my guest. I got you covered."

"It was already suggested to do that on the way here," Holmes said.

"Russ, you're an asshole for divulging. That was supposed to be top secret." Ferguson jokingly laid into his attaché.

All three men laughed heartily.

After the small talk was over, and they had enough alcohol in their systems to make the conversation flow easily, Ferguson got serious. "So what's your plan to get the OX312? You were pretty damned confident of success when we spoke on the phone."

"It's classified," Mueller answered, chuckling.

"Cut the bullshit. I have the highest security clearance that exists."

"Take it easy. I'm just pulling your leg. My operative has already made off with a vial of the experimental drug from Schaeffer's lab. A pal of mine who runs the intelligence operation at Gitmo couldn't say enough good things about it. Prisoners who have kept their traps shut for years start singing like birds and all without inflicting any pain or suffering. It's fucking amazing. Interrogation will never be the same."

"What about Schaeffer and his Asian chick associate? Are they going to sign it over to the agency?"

"We're still working on that aspect."

Mueller's speech was getting more slurred by the minute. He motioned Ferguson closer so he could whisper in his ear. "But if they don't do as we say, I'm afraid both of them may need to be neutralized."

"Fuckin' A!" Ferguson exclaimed, raising his drink for a toast as Mueller and Holmes did likewise.

"For God and country!" all three exclaimed as they downed their glasses to the last drop.

29

Angela had looked in the mirror and practiced her speech a dozen times, but standing outside Gabe's office, she wasn't sure she could go through with it. Only a few weeks ago, the thought of what she was about to do would have seemed impossible. However, now Angela was going to tell Gabe she was leaving Boston General to take a job working for Novara in Switzerland.

She opened the door and entered his office, hoping to maintain her confidence. Gabe was sitting behind his desk, but across from him was the cause of all her angst, Vanessa Trent.

"Oh, I'm sorry," Angela said. "I'll come back another time."

"No, that's OK," Gabe said. "Please stay. There is something important I want to tell you."

"Oh, what's that?" she asked softly, unsure of what was coming next.

"I'm going to give a lecture in Aspen and will be gone next week. Could you do me a huge favor, and fill in for the Springhill site visit next Tuesday?"

"Sure, that'll be just fine. I can manage that." Angela paused and took a breath before proceeding. "There's something I have to tell you as well." Angela's voice faltered. "I'm leaving Boston General."

"You're what!" Gabe exclaimed.

"I'm leaving."

"I don't understand."

"I took a position with Novara Pharmaceutical. I'm moving abroad the end of next week. In all likelihood I won't be here when you get back from your trip."

"When did you decide this? You never mentioned it to me." Gabe had a startled expression on his face. "I have to say, I'm totally floored."

Gabe and Angela were talking as if Vanessa weren't there. Meanwhile, she was taking the whole thing in, assessing the implications for her mission.

"Well, don't be so shocked," Angela told him. "The people at Novara are extremely supportive of my research and excited to have me join them. They are giving me my own staff and a pretty much unlimited budget."

"But, Angela, I—"

"Gabe, I apologize for not discussing this sooner, but my decision is final. I have to be moving on. I know you'll take good care of the inhabitants of Dodge City after I leave."

"Of course I will."

"And about funding, you needn't worry. The money from the check I deposited in our research account can stay. Novara has even given permission for you to continue using OX312 for the Springhill study."

"Well, thanks, that's very kind. But—"

Abruptly pivoting around, Angela headed out the door before Gabe had a chance to finish.

"Angela...," he called after her.

Gabe turned toward Vanessa with a quizzical look, then shrugged his shoulders and held his hands up in a gesture of utter amazement. He had just been thrown a huge curve ball, one he would never have expected in a million years.

Leaving the office, Angela rushed over to the research building lab. She went inside, locked the door, and burst into tears.

***

That evening Gabe wanted some time to himself to reflect on the day's events with Angela, so he made an excuse to Vanessa that he needed to work on his lecture for the Aspen meeting.

"No worries," she told him. "I've got to go shopping and pick up some things for the Aspen trip anyway."

Once Gabe was alone, he thought about Angela, recalling their night of passion and the years they had worked together. To have her leave like this was painful. Perhaps he hadn't spent enough time with Angela since Vanessa arrived and she felt neglected. *For God's sake, I'm a psychiatrist. I should have sensed Angela was unhappy and done something about it.* However, now it was too late. Angela's decision was made. She was leaving Boston General.

Gabe believed he was in love with Vanessa, but in truth didn't know much about her. She was gorgeous and intelligent. He delighted in her presence, but knew next to nothing about her past. Gabe had gone so far as to buy an engagement ring, planning to propose in Aspen. Was he moving too fast? Was this really love or just lust? For a moment he was struck by uncertainty. He knew an emotion as powerful as *love* had the ability to distort judgment. Had it blinded him? As a professional who routinely analyzed others he should have been able to understand his own feelings and motivation, but now questioned if he could be making a mistake.

In a few days he was leaving with Vanessa for Aspen, while Angela would be moving to Switzerland. When he returned to Boston, things would be very different without his dedicated research assistant around. He had collaborated with her every step of the way with OX312. As he reflected, Gabe realized that it was more than just the working together on OX312. He would miss Angela's gentle smile and soft touch, but his future was not with her, it was with Vanessa.

30

The flight over the Rockies was a bumpy one, but once on the ground, the turbulence was quickly forgotten. A cab took Gabe and Vanessa to their hotel, at the foot of Aspen Mountain. Instead of snow the ski runs were covered with green grass and blossoming flowers. Countless aspen pines lined the empty runs that streaked up the mountain, their leaves delightfully fluttering in the breeze.

"Why would anyone want to come here in the dead of winter?" Vanessa asked. "This place is like heaven on earth in the summer."

She had a mission to complete, but aside from that, Vanessa was having the best time of her life. She truly enjoyed the things Gabe did with her, from the sailing to his lovemaking. Vanessa couldn't help but feel that if the time ever came to settle down, it would be with a man like him.

After arrival at the hotel, Gabe wanted to make some modifications in his lecture, so the first day in Aspen, Vanessa was left to her own devices. While he worked on his computer, she walked through the town. There were no terrorists or saboteurs in Aspen, just people she saw spending their time living life to the fullest. A jazz festival was in progress, and walking the streets, music filled the air as clusters of musicians gathered to play at different spots all over the town.

Vanessa bought a cup of coffee and sat listening to the melodies floating in the air. She watched a group of young children with their mothers, playing in the park next to where she sat.

Suddenly thoughts buried deep inside rose to the surface. *What about children? Will I ever have them? I couldn't continue doing what I do, running all over the world and risking my life. Maybe a position as an analyst or a trainer for recruits would work.*

Vanessa was twenty-nine, and her biological clock was ticking. It had chosen this afternoon to give her a message as direct as the ones Mueller gave her before sending her out on missions.

At the same time those thoughts coursed through her head, instead of being conflicted, she felt the most relaxed she had been in a long time. Turning her face upward toward a cloudless azure sky, Vanessa sat back enjoying the warmth high-altitude solar radiance provided. *Perhaps it's time to think seriously about another role at the agency?*

Returning to the hotel, Vanessa was going to seduce Gabe into a brief midday sexual interlude, but instead was disappointed to find the room empty. There was a note on the desk. Vanessa picked it up and read:

Vanessa,
I had to go meet with the conference coordinator.
I will be back as soon as I can.
Love, Gabe

She went to her backpack, took out the secure phone, and walked out onto the balcony. Vanessa saw that a call had come in from Mueller only minutes before arriving back at the room.

"Alex will be delivering a package for you," his message curtly told her. "Meet him by the entrance to the gondola ski lift at sixteen thirty hours."

OK. But what's inside the package? Vanessa wondered. The gondola was only a few blocks from where they were staying. She could see it from the room balcony, coursing steeply up the face of the mountain. It still functioned during the summer, taking those sightseers and hikers who wanted a quicker, easier way up to the summit than a climb by foot for several hours.

Vanessa left the room and walked over to the gondola lift, standing near the base as instructed. At precisely the time indicated, a motorcycle pulled up on the street only a few hundred feet away. The rider was wearing a helmet that he didn't remove. She rushed down the stairs leading up to the gondola's base, and over to meet her contact. When he saw her approach, Alex pulled out a small package from his backpack and handed it to her.

"Special delivery from Mueller," was all he said. Then without even saying goodbye, he took off down the street on his motorcycle.

"From Mueller, from Mueller," she repeated to herself. She was so sick and tired of hearing that line. Alex could have stopped to say, "Hello, how are you?" or "How fucking lucky are we to be on assignment in Aspen?" But her contact was such a damn robot—all business, nothing else.

She immediately went into a nearby public bathroom and locked herself in a stall. Vanessa ripped open the package, anxious to see what Mueller had sent. Inside were two items. One was a military-grade GPS device, the other a 9mm pistol. She feverishly searched the package for a note with instructions, tearing it into pieces in the process, but there was none.

A GPS device and a gun. What did Mueller have in mind? Was there someone around that she needed to protect herself and Gabe from? Had the Russians or some other foreign power gotten wind of his discovery, and were they now after him? She held the weapon in her hand and examined it. The safety was on and its clip fully loaded. Vanessa was an expert marksman. If anybody was going to mess with them, they had better be prepared.

31

ngela stepped off the Novara company jet onto Swiss soil for the first time in her life. A limousine was waiting by the tarmac. It picked her up from the airfield, taking her to a residence Inger had scouted out, an apartment in Bern's city center. When Angela opened the door to where she would be living, she was aghast. It had to be at least three thousand square feet of fully furnished luxury dwelling in the heart of town. The view it offered was spectacular.

This is amazing, she thought. *What more could I ask for?* Angela saw a bouquet of flowers with a note on the kitchen table. Opening it, she read:

Dear Dr. Chen,

Make yourself comfortable in your new abode. Consider this apartment a gift from Paul Holfield and Novara for choosing to work with us. We look forward to seeing you at our office tomorrow. The refrigerator is stocked with food. Most things you might need to manage your new home are already there. Call my personal cell if you are in need of anything.

All the best,

Inger Kroll

Wow! Angela thought. *Who the heck needs Gabe Schaeffer and Boston General now?*

32

The only deficiency Gabe could find with Aspen was the lack of a nearby ocean on which to sail. However, the mountains offered other enticing opportunities. They went white-water rafting in the morning, and biked during the afternoon. Both were having great fun on the day before his presentation. For Gabe, thoughts of his patients or research quickly faded away. In Vanessa's case, Mueller and the agency might as well have been located on another planet.

They walked the streets of Aspen, enjoying the pleasant ambiance, occasionally stopping to view the expensive items in storefronts along their path.

"On my salary," Gabe confessed to Vanessa, "the only thing I can afford is looking."

They had dinner that evening at Mezzaluna, along with a nice bottle of Cabernet.

"Did you enjoy the meal?" the waiter asked before delivering the bill.

"It was superb," Gabe answered, while Vanessa nodded in complete agreement. They sat at the table holding hands and ogling each other like lovesick teenagers. After paying, when Gabe was walking out, he grabbed a box of matches from a bowl near the restaurant exit.

"Maybe we'll come back someday. This will help me remember," Gabe said, sticking the box of matches in his pocket.

"What about tomorrow?" she half-jokingly suggested, hugging his arm tightly as they began heading back toward their hotel.

A full moon overhead gave a shadowy outline to the towering peaks surrounding them. They were living a fairy tale, walking down an enchanting boulevard. Italian lights wrapped about the trees and stars glistened overhead.

For a moment Gabe thought this might be the right time for him to propose. Then he changed his mind. Gabe told himself to hold off until their hike up the mountain. What better place to ask Vanessa than on the summit of Aspen Mountain?

When they returned to their room, a full moon shone bright through the glass doors of their suite. Warm from their walk and the wine at dinner, Gabe headed over and opened them, letting the evening breeze enter. When he turned around, Vanessa was standing stark naked in front of him. She walked over and began taking off his shirt, kissing his chest as she undid the buttons. In seconds he too was undressed, and they were in bed, making love. Then she did something she would never dare permit with the men on other missions. She allowed Gabe to be on top. Sex during that position left her potentially vulnerable. However, her present lover posed no danger. Unlike the others, he was a dedicated physician, not a weapons dealer, an agent for a foreign government, or head of a drug cartel.

She relished the unusual sensation of her lover moving back and forth above her. Vanessa moaned softly with pleasure until both reached climax. Afterward they lay on the bed sheets moist with perspiration. She curled up into a ball in her lover's arms. He gently moved aside strands of hair that had fallen over her face. Vanessa sighed softly, utterly contented.

They fell asleep with the balcony doors open. The drapes on either side undulated to the gentle mountain breeze.

Vanessa thought she heard a sound in the darkness. She got up from bed and walked into the living room. She felt anxious. Something was bothering her. Her steps were tentative as if the next might plunge her into a deep hole. She was surprised to see her father, in his full dress uniform, sitting there. His chest was covered with decorations for service and valor.

"Daddy, can I sit on your lap?" she asked softly.

"Sure, come on over honey."

He took off his hat and laid it on the lamp table next to the sofa where he sat, then held his arms out for her.

She climbed up on his lap. "Daddy," she said, "I'm so scared."

"Of what?" he asked.

"I don't know, but I'm afraid."

"Sweetheart, I've had many enemies try to kill me, and here I am. It's my job to protect everybody else, especially you. So you don't have to be afraid of anything."

Pamela nestled in her father's arms. Suddenly, there was a hard knock at the door. It opened, and a soldier carrying an M-16 peered in.

"Sir," he said, "your men are waiting."

"I'll be a moment," Colonel Carter told the soldier.

He picked his daughter up and placed her gently down at his side. He took his hat and positioned it on his head, then straightened his uniform.

Carter saluted Pamela and left her sitting alone on the sofa as the door closed shut behind him.

Vanessa awoke in a sweat, her heart pounding. It was three thirty in the morning. She felt unsettled. *Weird dream,* Vanessa thought, *must be the altitude.* But it was more than that. She had the same dream before. In moments the images that were so vivid began to grey, and it became increasingly difficult to recall what was just experienced. Soon the entire nocturnal visit with her father disappeared into subconsciousness.

Gabe was still sleeping, but she turned to him and began caressing his body. He responded, and pulled her toward him. Half-asleep, Gabe again made love to Vanessa. Afterward, as he held her, Gabe's reassuring touch relieved the inner tension Vanessa's dream had produced, and she fell soundly asleep for the balance of the night.

First thing in the morning Gabe left for the conference prepared to make his presentation while Vanessa was still in bed. She got up late, but still felt tired after her restive night. Her secure phone suddenly rang, and she jumped with a start, running over to pick it up. It was Mueller.

"Is it safe to talk?" he asked.

"Yes, I'm alone." Her heart started to beat faster. She didn't want her fantasy time with Gabe to end, but she had the feeling that what Mueller was about to tell her would rip it all to shreds.

"They need to be neutralized," Mueller said without emotion in his voice.

"Who needs to be *neutralized?*" she asked, afraid of the answer.

"Both Schaeffer and Chen."

Vanessa's spirit sank. "But, I'm sure I can convince him to—"

Mueller interrupted. "There is no other option. The determination has been made. I want you to take care of it today. Alex will pick you up afterward and take you to Denver. From there you fly back to DC. Chen has moved to Switzerland, so you will have to go there next. Let's plan on a get-together once you are back in DC for further instructions."

The line went dead. Vanessa remained in shock, still standing with the phone against her ear. Then she suddenly came back to life, throwing it against the wall, and breaking the phone into pieces.

Vanessa went into the closet, closed the door, and screamed at the top of her lungs, "Fuuuuck!" Then she fell to her knees in the darkness and sobbed.

When Gabe returned from the conference, he was in an upbeat mood, believing he had done a gangbuster job with his lecture, but found Vanessa strangely silent.

"In case you're wondering," he told her, "my presentation was very well received."

"That's great," she said halfheartedly.

"Those who attended now understand it's possible to deal with episodic violence the same way as with other psychiatric disorders. I couldn't be happier." He smiled from ear to ear. "Well, are you ready for our hike?"

"Sure, let's go," Vanessa answered. "I packed some energy bars and water bottles in the backpacks."

"OK, let me change quickly, then we'll take off."

After they left the hotel room, Gabe paused. "Oops, I forgot something. I'll only be a second." He ran back to the room, went to his suitcase, and found a small black box hidden inside. Gabe opened it to make sure the ring was still there. Its diamond sparkled brilliantly. Yes, he was certain. Once they reached the end of their hike up Aspen Mountain, Gabe would get down on one knee and propose. He couldn't wait to see the look on Vanessa's face.

33

The hotel's van drove them to the back of Aspen Mountain and let them off near the start of a trailhead that went up the mountain's backside. Gabe thanked the driver and tipped him ten dollars. As the vehicle drove off, they started their upward trek.

The weather was absolutely perfect, just cool enough for a demanding hike. They began their ascent at just over eight thousand feet of elevation. For two persons recently arriving from sea level that were not yet fully acclimatized to altitude, climbing the mountain would be challenging in spite of their being in good condition. About one mile from the starting point, Vanessa took Gabe off the main trail leading him onto a path through the woods. "According to the map this should be a less steep up this way," she said with confidence.

Above nine thousand feet there were still traces of residual winter snow in shady spots. The view from a meadow they entered was exceptional. It gave them a panoramic view of the Rockies for as far as the eye could see. They stopped briefly, drank some water, ate an energy bar, then continued onward until they reached a fork.

"Gabe, let's head to the right. I spoke with the hotel concierge earlier, and he told me it's a more scenic route to the summit."

"Sure, you show me the way."

Vanessa bounded ahead, and Gabe struggled to keep up. He was amazed at the shape she was in.

"Honey, can you hold on a minute? I need to stop and rest." Gabe took the bottle from his backpack. After gulping down some water he held it out toward Vanessa. "Want some?"

"No, I'm not thirsty." She answered curtly, then urged him, "Come on, we should keep on going." Vanessa marched ahead as Gabe struggled to keep pace.

They kept on the trail, which progressively became rougher and narrower. Gabe kept following Vanessa, placing his trust in her as guide. They crossed a mountain stream, hopping across the big rocks to the other side. The tall pines blocked the direction of the sun. Gabe was drenched in sweat and becoming seriously fatigued.

"How much longer do you think till we get to the top?"

"It shouldn't be much further," she answered, keeping up her fast pace.

Gabe was near total exhaustion. Each step was increasingly difficult. He just wanted to reach the damned summit. They were no longer on anything that resembled a well trodden path while making their way through the rough mountainous terrain.

Entering another clearing, Gabe said, "Hold on, I've got to stop, or I'll pass out." He bent over with hands on his knees, gasping for air, sweat dripping down his face. When he recovered enough to stand erect, Gabe turned to Vanessa, ready to admit that she was undoubtedly the better hiker of the two. Then he noticed the serious stone-cold look on her face that had nothing to do with fatigue.

"What's up, Vanessa? Is something wrong?"

She took off her backpack and reached inside. Gabe thought she was getting a water bottle. Instead, she pulled out a gun.

Gabe laughed. "Are you going to shoot me because I'm not fast enough?"

"This is no joke, Gabe. The gun is real." He was confused and didn't know what to think. Vanessa's actions were beyond imaginable.

"Gabe, I'm not a psychologist. I work for a government agency that thinks OX312 is too dangerous to allow you to continue using it, and they don't want anyone else getting their hands on it."

"No, this can't be happening. It can't be true." Gabe shook his head in disbelief.

"Gabe, I really care for you…I'm in love with you, but you have to understand I have my orders."

"What orders?"

"Gabe, just agree to give them the drug, and forget OX312 exists. Tell me that, Gabe, and I guarantee everything will be OK."

"Vanessa, the drug can help prevent violent crimes. It will keep innocent people from getting hurt. Our prisons are overflowing with men and women who don't have to be there and could otherwise lead productive lives, if they just had this treatment."

"This is not my call, Gabe. The people I work for are much smarter than I. They have analyzed the situation and made the decision. The drug has to be in their hands. Just say yes, Gabe. Please, say *yes* to me!"

"I can't do that. I could never do that. As much as I love you, Vanessa, I simply can't do what you ask."

She tried not to think, and tried even harder not to feel. "Gabe, I'll have no choice but to shoot you if you don't cooperate. I mean it. Damn you, don't be so stubborn."

"Look, I want to show you something." He opened his backpack and took out the small black box. Gabe opened it so she could see the diamond ring inside. "I was going to ask you, Vanessa Trent, or whoever the hell you really are, to be my wife!"

Gabe was standing less than twenty feet away from the woman he wanted to marry…a woman who now held a gun on him, told him she loved him, but threatened to shoot him.

Her hand was trembling so badly, she didn't know if the bullet would hit its mark. Suddenly, a vision of Mueller appeared standing next to Gabe. He looked impatient, waiting for her to act.

She held back hoping for Gabe to change his mind, but his facial expression showed total defiance. Finally, she screamed at the top of her lungs, "I love you!" just before squeezing the trigger. The sound of the gunshot rang out as the bullet hit Gabe. Its force knocked him off his feet and he fell backward onto the ground. For a while Gabe lay there semiconscious. When he came to, Gabe slowly pulled himself to a sitting position and looked around. Vanessa was gone.

He had a stinging pain in his thigh. The bullet had gone clean through the flesh, but fortunately hadn't hit bone or artery. It hurt like hell, but wasn't fatal. It would have been so simple for her to kill him if she really wanted, but it was obvious that at the last second, she decided not to. Nonetheless, Gabe figured his life was still in grave danger. It would be dark in an hour. The temperature was already starting to drop. What were his chances of getting off the mountain alive? He would probably die of hypothermia, if not blood loss, before the night was over. Gabe took off his belt and cinched it around his thigh to slow the bleeding. As he cinched the belt, Gabe felt something in his pant pocket and reached inside. It was the box of matches he took leaving the restaurant the night before.

Gabe found a large branch to use for support. He hobbled around the clearing gathering underbrush and dry wood. Gabe put it in a pile, got down on his knees, and lit a match. Smoke started to rise. He blew into the smoldering brush and prayed the fire would take.

Two miles away a forest ranger was stationed at his post. The weather had been unusually dry, and the fire risk for campers was posted as high. No campfires would be allowed until the next rain. Every half hour the ranger scanned the horizon with his binoculars. Then he saw it, smoke rising in the distance. He picked up the phone and called ground patrol.

"Some moron started a fire near the top of west ridge. I see a dense plume of smoke coming up through the treetops. Go over there and have them put it out right away before the whole mountainside goes up in flames."

"But that location isn't near any approved camping site." The ranger on patrol noted, then continued. "I'll take whoever started that fire to Sheriff Collins at Ashcroft. He'll fine the shit out of them or throw them in jail overnight."

Shadows were growing long when the ranger patrol arrived. The temperature had dropped twenty degrees from its afternoon peak. Instead of a camper, the patrol found Gabriel Schaeffer, who managed to stand up, using his branch as support, just before he collapsed.

The patrol leader helped revive him. Seeing blood all over the injured man's pants, and what appeared to be a bullet hole, the ranger asked, "What happened? Did a hunter accidentally shot you?"

"Well, it wasn't exactly a hunter and not exactly an accident."

The rangers who found Gabe put out the fire, and called for a helicopter rescue on their satellite phone. Gabe shook hands and thanked them before the door was slammed shut, and the chopper took off for the regional medical center.

***

When Vanessa didn't show up at the designated pickup location by the gondola, Alex was concerned. He called Mueller.

"Something must be wrong. She's over a half hour late, and she's never late."

"Alex, just be patient. There's no need to panic."

The sun went down, and still no sign of her. Alex didn't see any point to waiting longer. He drove off.

Early next morning after she didn't return his call on the secure phone, Alex turned on his GPS. He saw a transponder signal coming from far in the backcountry behind Aspen Mountain, but it was stationary. *What the hell?* Alex headed out to find Vanessa. He took along his own gun just in case.

After hours of hiking, he was closing in on her location. Then Alex spotted a gnarled backpack lying on the ground. Inside he found the functioning GPS still emitting its signal, and an envelope. There was no sign of his partner.

34

Mueller called Ferguson over at Defense. "I think we're fucked, or at least I'm fucked," he said with a tone of resignation.

"What are you talking about?" Ferguson asked.

"The female agent I had handling Schaeffer was supposed to neutralize him, but never showed up at the rendezvous spot with her contact."

"Maybe she was having such a good time on the assignment that she forgot."

"Hardly, she was the best agent I had."

"What's with the past tense?"

"She had a contact who tracked her location using his GPS. He hiked through rough mountain terrain near Aspen for hours before finding a backpack with the government-issue GPS I had sent her. However, the agent was nowhere to be found, and hasn't contacted me since."

"So what's the problem? With Schaeffer eliminated, I'm sure you can find another operative to take her place, and get rid of the Asian lady."

"You don't understand. Let me finish."

"Inside the backpack, along with the GPS, was a letter addressed to me. Apparently, she was planning to give it to her contact and have him pass it along. I'll read it to you."

"I'm all ears."

I have worked for the agency since my career began. I'm certain you realize the sacrifices inherent in the kind of work I do and the dedication to our country it required. Unfortunately, I have to tender my resignation effective immediately. Dr. Schaeffer has agreed to terminate all work on OX312 and forget it ever existed.

My only request is that you leave Dr. Schaeffer and me alone. Should any harm come to either of us, a document detailing the CIA's illegal interference in civilian affairs will be delivered to the chairman of the Senate Oversight Committee for government intelligence. If we are left in peace, it will remain our secret.

Agent Pamela Carter

"Shit," Ferguson exclaimed, "she fell in love with her target."

"It certainly looks that way."

"Unfortunately, the fucking letter she spoke about is a total wildcard. It could be on the way to the Senate as we speak."

"So what's the next move?"

"A little preemptive action is in order. There's no way I can hang around here with some love crazed agent dangling a sword over my head. I submitted my resignation to the agency earlier today. A week from now, I will be fishing at my place in Key Largo. My army pension plus the agency retirement package should be enough to keep me comfortable for the rest of my days. If history is any guide, they don't go after us if we leave the agency before shit hits the fan."

"What's my exposure?" Ferguson asked, sounding worried.

"Little to none. You should be fine. She worked for me, not for you."

"Next question. When can I come visit your place in Florida?"

"Anytime you want. Just bring your own suntan lotion. I'll provide the fishing poles and beer."

"Then expect to see me soon," Ferguson told his friend as he put down the phone. He felt relieved after hearing Mueller's assurance about his not being caught up in any scandal that might evolve.

Ferguson picked up the large file that lay in front of him on his desk that he had been reviewing before Mueller's call. There was still serious work to be done before the work day ended. His department was in the midst of finalizing its budget request for next year. He and Holmes would be staying up late to finalize the details.

Ferguson buzzed his attaché in his office down the corridor. "Can you bring the spreadsheets so we can go over the numbers?"

"Sure, sir, I'll be there momentarily."

Holmes came into Ferguson's office carrying a bundle of files. "I have it all here, sir."

"Great."

Ferguson began looking over the complicated data sheets. "Damn, going through all this is going to take hours."

Holmes spoke, "Sir, I hope you don't mind, I took the liberty of ordering dinner for us since I knew we would working late."

"That's what I like about you, Holmes, you think of everything."

Ferguson's attaché beamed from his boss's acknowledgment. Later that evening a staff member from the kitchen rolled in a dinner cart, set up the portable table, and arranged the place settings.

"Anything else I can get for you gentleman?"

"A bottle of vodka," Ferguson jokingly quipped.

"No, we're set," Holmes said. "You can pick this up in the morning."

The attaché tipped the man, who appreciatively thanked him and left the room.

"What do we have for our feast?" Ferguson asked.

"I ordered rack of lamb with potatoes au gratin."

"My favorite," the colonel exclaimed. "All right, let's dig in. I'm famished."

Ferguson took his seat at the table and lifted the silver cover off his plate. "This looks fantastic. Say, Holmes, why not be a good boy and fix me a Johnny Walker straight up."

"It would be a pleasure, sir." Holmes went to the closet. He knew exactly where Ferguson kept his stash of booze for special occasions.

"Make mine a double and go ahead and make one for yourself," Ferguson said. "If we're going to be stuck in here all night, we might as well make it enjoyable."

Holmes went to the closet in the far corner of the expansive office where Ferguson's bar was located. As the colonel began eating his dinner, the attaché made drinks.

Holmes made the colonel his double scotch. Then he did something he had been planning to do when the opportunity arose. Holmes added some OX312 to his superior officer's drink, and a small amount to his own.

***

Lieutenant Holmes had no trouble on his next attempt to get some of the drug from Schaeffer's lab. This time he dressed up as a security guard and pretended to be making his rounds. When he went inside the lab, he headed straight to the storage safe. Holmes tinkered with a code analysis device he brought along until it registered. The safe door clicked open, and he carefully removed a small amount of the drug from one of the vials, putting it into his own container. Afterward, Holmes locked the safe and left. Nobody would ever know about his second visit.

***

About two hours after dinner and another round of drinks, both Holmes and his boss were feeling good, in spite of the work they still had left in front of them.

"When you add all the numbers up, we're thirty million over projections. Fuck! I'll probably get dinged for overspending, and they'll hold my advancement to brigadier."

Holmes saw the worried look on his boss's face. He put his hand gently on Ferguson's shoulder and said, "Please don't be so upset. I'm sure I can tweet the numbers so they comes out on target." Then Holmes looked at Ferguson and felt the uncontrollable urge to do something. He kissed him on the lips.

Ferguson pulled away, mortified, wiping his lips off with his the sleeve of his shirt He glared at Holmes, his face turning red.

"I'm sorry, sir, but I've wanted to do that for a very long time," Holmes said. "I hope you feel the same way I do."

"You're a goddamned fag, aren't you? I wondered about that, and now I know. Get the hell out of my office!"

Holmes was shocked by the fury of Ferguson's response and didn't understand how it was possible. *I gave him a dose of OX312 in his drink. Why is he acting like this?* What Holmes didn't realize was that he had mistakenly taken the look-alike placebo instead of the real drug.

"Sir, I'm sorry. I don't know what got into me. It's probably the alcohol. Please forgive me."

Ferguson laid into him again. "Get the fuck out of here before I rip you apart. I can't believe I didn't realize it before. I've got a *homo* working for me."

Ferguson stood up and pushed his attaché away. Holmes tripped and fell to the floor, then slowly got up on his hands and knees. The attaché looked up at the man he had loved for so long, who had just utterly rejected him.

"But sir, I love you," Holmes pleaded.

"You sick motherfucker. Get out, and don't let me see you around here again. If I do, I'll kill you."

Holmes stood up and straightened the hair that had fallen over his face. He was trying hard not to cry but couldn't help it. The attaché adjusted his uniform, then saluted Ferguson and left his office. Walking like a zombie down the corridor to his own office, he went inside and locked the door. Holmes needed to be alone.

Taking some paper, he began to write. Ferguson's attaché told the story of OX312 and how his superior officer had ordered him to stealing it. He wiped the tears from his eyes and blew his nose. Finally, Holmes got up from the desk and went to his closet, opening the door. His full-dress military uniform hung there and next to it, a holster with a gun. Holmes pulled the service revolver out. He sat back down at his desk, opened his mouth, put the gun barrel inside, then pulled the trigger. Blood and brains splattered over the Defense Department wall behind him.

The years of torment and paranoia about being a gay man in the military were over.

35

Three men sat in the office of Hans Roessler, Inspector General at FEDPOL, a Swiss equivalent of the FBI. Investigators Arturo Gonzales traveled from Mexico City, and Nels Halper, of Interpol, had come from Brussels. Roessler sat behind his desk waiting to hear what his foreign guests had to say. Halper began their conversation.

"Mr. Roessler, we have spent the last three years tracking the movements of a man named George Fleming. His story is a remarkable one. Born in England, he received a PhD at Oxford in biochemistry, then did postdoctoral work at MIT. Subsequently, he moved to Mazatlan, Mexico. I won't belabor you with the details, but he was an integral part of a group involved in organ theft and illegal human research. While working there he was responsible for the deaths of several individuals to whom he personally administered experimental medications that caused fatal complications.

"After Mexico, Fleming fled to Costa Rica, where he underwent plastic surgery that altered his face, and he assumed a new identity as the Canadian citizen Paul Holfield. He then traveled to Africa, taking a job directing field research for Celestica, a Swiss pharmaceutical company. Just before Celestica went insolvent, Fleming joined up with his current firm, Novara. There he quickly rose in the ranks to become the firm's vice chairman. That is the story of the man who now calls himself Paul Holfield."

"You are absolutely right, Mr. Halper, that is quite a tale."

"Interpol has an outstanding warrant for his arrest. Mr. Gonzales is here to take him back to Mexico City, where he will stand trial for murder and various crimes against humanity."

At the mention of the words, "crimes against humanity," Hans Roessler cringed. The Swiss were particularly sensitive on that issue. Over half a century after world war two, evidence continued to come out about Swiss banks participating in handling assets for the Third Reich, including gold, jewelry, and artworks confiscated from victims of the Holocaust. There were also annoying instances of Swiss banks exposed for hiding the fortunes of dictators who stole from their own oppressed people. The last thing Roessler wanted was a new story about a business magnate high up in the vaunted Swiss firm, Novara, accused of *crimes against humanity*. He cringed to think of the embarrassing headlines in the international press.

"How can you be so sure Paul Holfield and George Fleming are the same person?" Roessler asked.

Halper pulled out a file from his briefcase and laid it on Roessler's desk.

"You can see for yourself," Halper said, "that although the facial portraits of Fleming and Holfield look so different, their fingerprints are exactly alike. There is no doubt that Paul Holfield and George Fleming, are in fact, the very same person."

Gonzales, who had been sitting quietly, began to speak. "Let me add this, Mr. Roessler. Fleming is a totally despicable individual. He experimented on the poor people of Mazatlan strictly for monetary gain. We have been trying to find him for a very long time. It was really a fluke that we were able to locate him."

"What do you mean, a fluke?" Roessler queried.

"It seems Mr. Holfield, while doing business in Las Vegas, visited with a known prostitute. About three months ago, this hooker was arrested for possession of cocaine. Rather than face a long jail sentence, she gave authorities the names of clients she suspected might be in trouble with the law. One of those names was that of George Fleming, aka Paul Holfield. If it weren't for that hooker's information, Fleming might never have been found."

"I see," Roessler said. He realized Fleming's crimes could not be ignored, but he also knew it might take time to get things resolved. "Gentlemen, unfortunately we have a very complicated set of extradition laws here in Switzerland. I'm afraid it may take some time and the involvement of lawyers to resolve the issue of sending him back to Mexico."

"But didn't Holfield enter this country using a fake Canadian passport?" Halper asked. "Unless I'm mistaken, you have the legal right to deport him immediately."

"In that regard I believe you are correct," Roessler answered, smiling. He was just as happy to avoid the agony of a protracted legal battle over extradition and the media attention that would accompany it. "From my standpoint I will try to resolve this matter as quickly as possible and without involving the press."

"We understand," Halper answered, nodding his head in affirmation along with Gonzales.

"Good, then let's discuss our plan of attack."

36

After she shot the man she loved, Pamela ran crying and stumbling along the mountain. She felt like a complete failure in every respect. Pamela not only didn't succeed in convincing Gabe to see things her way, but then couldn't bring herself to shoot and kill him as ordered. Even without making the easy fatal shot to his head, she feared he might still die. The wound in the thigh would prevent him from walking. When the sun went down the temperature would plummet and turn freezing cold. Gabe could die of hypothermia. Pamela was beside herself in anguish.

Suddenly, as she fought her way along the rough terrain, a solution popped into her head. *I'll go back for him. I could get some fake passports, and we could escape to Mexico or Mozambique, anywhere else in the world.* But, even as Pam's heart told her to go back, she knew that it would be no use. Mueller would track them down and kill them wherever they went.

Pamela walked by a steep cliff and thought of putting an end to the struggle going on in her head by jumping off. Instead, she stopped at the edge and threw her gun as far as she could over the precipice, continuing on, with tears running down her face.

She halted to take her backpack off and look at the GPS. *Only three miles from a road.* Once Pam reached it, she would hitch a ride back to town. Later, Alex would pick her up, and it would be all over, except in her mind. Pam could never forget pulling the trigger and shooting the only man she loved, and for what? Did she do it out of blind dedication to Mueller, or to satisfy her father's legacy of patriotic service? What did she have left now but the empty slogan she'd heard a thousand times before? "*For God and for country.*" What true God or worthy country would have sanctioned what she just did?

Putting the GPS inside her backpack, she suddenly froze as something up ahead rustled in the underbrush. She listened. Maybe it was another hiker who got lost? In the quiet of the forest that surrounded her, Pamela heard what sounded like a kitten's meow. Out from behind a tree in front of her, a cat appeared. It stopped and stared at her in curiosity. It seemed the kitten had never before seen a human face. Pamela thought it looked like a large house cat but a little bulkier and with a tawny coat. For a moment she forgot her grief and wanted to step forward and pet it.

Mountain lions typically avoid all contact with humans. They stay away from well-traveled hiking trails and rarely if ever venture into campsites to forage for food like bears. Yet the Aspen rangers knew from recent sightings, from tracks they'd seen, and from the carcasses of dead animals that a mountain lion was roaming the area.

Suddenly, Pamela heard a growl that wasn't coming from the kitten. Just beyond the small feline, its mother, a full-size mountain lioness, came into view. Seeing an intruder who might harm her cub, the lioness's demeanor immediately turned aggressive. It snarled, then slowly crept forward, walking past her offspring. Now less than twelve feet from Pam, the cat snarled again, this time baring her sharp one-and-a-half-inch long canines.

The lioness leapt into the air. One hundred and thirty pounds of flying muscle knocked Pamela to the ground with a loud thud, forcing the air out of her lungs. The cat's claws tore at her arms and face as she tried in vain to protect herself. Nothing Pamela had learned in her close combat courses at the CIA prepared her for unarmed battle with a mountain lion. Finally, the lioness sank its teeth deep into Pamela's throat and wouldn't let go. Her last thought was, *Like that fucking Mueller, it won't let go.*

37

In the early morning before she went on her hike with Gabe, Pamela had called her aunt. She hadn't spoken with Aunt Betty in over a year. Pamela's missions prevented contact with anyone who might connect with her true identity, but now she was making an exception.

"Hello, Betty. It's me, Pamela," she said excitedly.

"Honey, it's been so long this time. I'm glad to hear your voice."

Pamela fought back tears, then told her, "I know, but it's not going to be that way much longer."

"What do you mean?"

"I'm quitting the agency, or at least the kind of work I do for them after my current assignment."

"Oh."

"Yes, I've met this wonderful man and fallen for him head over heels. I'm sure you'll like him when you meet. But I have to ask you for a big favor."

"Of course my dear, anything."

"I'm sending you an important letter for this friend of mine, a lawyer. If you don't hear from me during the next week, it's because my current mission is ending up taking longer than expected. In that event I want you to mail it to him. Will you do that favor for me?"

"Of course I will."

Pamela lied. If she didn't call Betty back within seven days, it would be because something bad had happened. She and Gabe would have to go into deep hiding if Mueller gave her a hard time about leaving the job with the target of her mission. Then her aunt would send the letter off, and they would have to wait until Mueller was thrown out of the agency before it would be safe to resurface.

"Betty, I've got to go now. I'm putting my letter to you in the mail right after getting off the phone. I love you, Auntie."

"Love you too, sweetheart, and take good care."

"Thanks again, and good-bye," Pamela said, hanging up.

**

Betty received a FedEx packet from the niece who had lived with her on and off as a child whenever her brother traveled abroad on his tours of duty.

Aunt Betty did just as Pamela had requested. Not hearing anything during the week that followed, she forwarded the enclosed envelope to a name and address scribbled on the piece of paper she found inside. When the letter arrived at the office of Pam's personal attorney in DC, he followed his client's instructions, seeing to it that her letter was hand delivered to the senator in charge of the Intelligence Oversight Committee in Congress.

**

It was a beautiful day in the Keys, not a cloud in the sky and calm waters. Mueller was out fishing in the bay when two US marshals pulled up alongside on a speedboat. The recently retired agency man put down his rod, but not the cold can of beer he had been drinking.

"Hey guys, what's up?" Mueller asked.

"Just a little special delivery item from Uncle Sam," one of the officers answered. He handed Mueller an envelope, and had him sign a receipt.

"Mind if we have one?" The marshal asked, pointing to the beer.

"Sure. It's a hot one today. "Mueller answered, tossing two beers from his cooler over to the officers. After the marshals shoved off, Mueller opened the envelope and began reading the documents inside. Seconds later he screamed, "Fuck me!" then threw the beer can he was holding far into the bay.

The marshals had served him with a subpoena to testify before the Senate Intelligence Oversight Committee.

***

During his closed-door hearing William Mueller was relentlessly chastised by both its Democratic and Republican committee members. He was subsequently censured. The CIA, the agency to which Mueller had dedicated much of his government career, punished him by terminating his pension and giving him a dishonorable discharge from its service.

38

During her time in Bern, Angela found the capital city of Switzerland a charming place to live. It was far away from Boston, and she got a bit homesick at times, but being there helped her to forget about working at the General, and especially about Gabriel Schaeffer. She was committed to a fresh start. Her clinical research project would soon be underway, and she had all the support a substantial company like Novara could muster. The plan was to aim for speedy data collection and submission to the European Medicines Agency for OX312 as a therapeutic agent within the year.

Holfield showed a special interest in Angela's work, and the commercialization of OX312 was one of his top priorities. During the last meeting she had with him, Holfield told her, "Angela, I have good news for you. Our marketing department has come up with a name for your medication. We couldn't very well continue to call it OX312 when it appears on the shelves of pharmacies and expect anyone to use it."

Angela chuckled at his joke as Holfield went on. "Marketing wants to call it *Aphrodesia,* after the Greek goddess of love, Aphrodite, if you agree."

"Sure, that sounds fine," she answered.

"Good, then it's settled." Holfield called his administrative assistant over the intercom. "Inger, have some champagne brought to the office and please join us. We are going to congratulate Dr. Chen on the future success of our newest drug, *Aphrodesia.*"

Turning to Angela, Holfield said, "Oh, one more thing. Our director of marketing wants to meet with you. He has a few questions before our advertizing campaign begins."

"Of course, I would be happy to, but isn't that a bit premature? We have a long ways to go with the clinical study."

"That may be true, but if we waited until everything was complete, we'd end up behind the veritable eight ball. With new drugs, we must have forward momentum, meaning marketplace interest before official approval and its appearance in local pharmacies."

Inger made Angela an appointment with the director of marketing the following week. When she entered his office, he said to her, "I've heard so many good things about you from Holfield. He's crazy about this new drug you've come up with that makes people love each other."

"Well, I wouldn't exactly put it that way. I'd rather say it induces positive feelings, promoting compassion and communication between people."

"Good. I like that." He jotted something down on his notepad. "So this agent helps people having problems with their loving relationships, correct?"

"Yes."

"Who are the persons you see needing to take the medication?"

"Only couples having serious marital problems."

"Oh?" The director of marking said, sounding surprised by her response. "Now let me ask you this. What do you think about all the people out there looking for love? Do you see them as a target group that would use the drug? Let's say you want a relationship with someone who isn't paying much attention to you so you buy some Aphrodesia and try it out on that person."

"No way, absolutely not! Laypeople shouldn't be using this drug unsupervised. The emotion of love is much too powerful to fool around with. Only licensed professionals, like psychologists or psychiatrists, should be allowed to prescribe it, and then under circumstances of couples having marital problems that require therapy."

"For your information, Dr. Chen, our focus group study on Aphrodesia indicated that persons looking for an intense love relationship outside of marriage represent a much larger potential market. Based on this data, its use in that group would dwarf the psychotherapeutic use in married couples. Our statistics demonstrate this fact quite definitively."

"I could never stand for that," Angela declared.

"Mr. Holfield has already authorized our marketing campaign to concentrate on just that group."

"No, you can't be serious."

"But I am. You mean he didn't tell you?"

Angela was angry. In fact, she was fuming. "No, he didn't say a single word about this to me. If he had, I would have told him I'm taking my OX312 and going back to Boston."

"I don't think you can do that."

"And why is that?"

"The rights to Aphrodesia were signed over to Novara. You no longer have any say in the matter."

"Like hell I don't!" Angela felt her face turning red with anger. "There is no way I can go along with this. No fucking way, understand?"

Angela turned around and stormed out of the marketing director's office. She did not plan to return. In fact, Angela was planning to do precisely as she had said—pack up and head back to Boston.

39

Paul Holfield was lying naked underneath a sheet on a massage table, getting his treatment. He was intermittently dozing off during the session. Magda, his favorite masseuse, was attending to each of the muscles in his back. They were stiff from his ride from Bern all the way to Lake Geneva, where the spa at hotel Le Chateau was located. By the time the therapist finished, he expected to feel like a new man.

Paul and Inger visited Le Chateau frequently. It was a few hours from the Novara headquarters in Bern and always provided a welcome escape. Le Chateau offered the privacy Paul relished, and the luxurious style to which both were accustomed.

Holfield's face was supported on the donut-hole cushion at the front of the table. An aromatic candle was burning, and a soothing Chopin nocturne played in the background. He was just dozing off when he noticed Magda had stopped kneading his shoulders and neck. He heard her go to the sink and wash her hands. Then the door to the darkened therapy room opened and closed. As he lay there, he thought, *She must have gone to get some hot stones.*

Paul loved the treatment she gave by placing smooth heated stones strategically on his back. Suddenly, the music stopped. He opened his eyes, looked down at the floor through the donut-hole his face was resting on, and saw a pair of black men's shoes.

"What the hell?" Paul said, pulling himself up to look. He found himself surrounded by men with serious expressions, all wearing police uniforms.

"George Fleming," one of the men said, "I have a warrant for your arrest."

Paul's heart practically jumped out of his chest. "George Fleming?" he said, wrapping the towel around his waist as he sat up. "Who in the blazes is George Fleming?"

"That, sir, would be you," another man answered.

The first man spoke again. "Please come with us now and without making any disturbance. Otherwise we will be forced to shackle and gag you. Le Chateau staff has requested that the atmosphere of their spa not be disturbed for the other clients."

Hans Roessler at FEDPOL decided that confronting Fleming at his office in the Novara headquarters would create too much of a scene. Gustav Jung, the CEO, was apprised of the situation and insisted Holfield be removed immediately, but with as little public fanfare as possible. Seeing a company director led out by police would result in a media circus within no time. Requests for interviews and details would follow. A major scandal would erupt, and damage control was one of Jung's priorities.

So Roessler had Jung's blessing to arrest Fleming on his weekly trip to Le Chateau, then make his extradition as private an affair as possible.

Roessler held up his warrant in front of Fleming. "This document outlines the crimes you are accused of committing, and the list is long. I will spare you the discomfort of reading through it all now. There will be ample time for you to review the indictment on your flight to Mexico City."

"Mexico City!" Fleming blurted out.

"That's where you're leaving for once you put your pants on."

"I want to call my lawyer immediately!" Fleming shouted indignantly.

"There will be no lawyers, Mr. Fleming. You entered this country illegally using a fraudulent Canadian passport and identity. We have every legal right to deport you whenever we wish, and that would be now."

"I can't leave the country without my passport," Fleming said.

"I'm sorry, but that passport is now impounded as evidence. You will not need a passport for the flight you are about to take, I can assure you."

Fleming got up slowly of the massage table and dressed. The angry look initially on his face was replaced by a sullen expression of resignation. He was led to a sedan waiting outside the back door of Le Chateau. Fleming didn't say another word on the way to the airport, realizing full well his life as a free man was over.

Two hours later he was on a flight to Mexico City and out of Hans Roessler's hair. Fleming knew what he was in for once he returned to Mexico, and he wasn't happy about it. They didn't have capital punishment, but that was of small comfort. He would be sentenced to life and slowly rot away in a godforsaken Mexican jail. There Fleming would have to remain in solitary confinement; otherwise, when the inmates got wind of his role at the Jamison Institute in Mazatlan, he was as good as dead. The charmed existence George Fleming had lived until now was over.

**

Inger was waiting for Paul in their suite at Le Chateau. She returned from her brief shopping expedition in the quaint local town that had its origins in the Middle Ages. The doorbell to their room rang, but instead of Paul Holfield, it was a hotel staff person delivering a cart with beluga caviar and champagne, which she had ordered earlier.

Inger patiently waited for her partner. As time passed, her hunger got the better of her. *Why not start without him? He is the one running late.* Inger took a wedge of toast and placed a generous spoonful of the caviar on top, with a small dollop of sour cream and a little chopped egg white, then took a bite.

"Ummm," she said. Then she poured herself a glass of champagne and one for Paul, anticipating he would show up at any moment, but Paul never arrived.

40

Gabriel Schaeffer was back at Boston General doing what he loved most: teaching, taking care patients, and doing research. He had a limp from the gunshot wound, but was making a quick physical recovery. The emotional healing would take a lot longer. He still missed Vanessa and wished things had turned out very differently.

When he left work that evening, Gabe decided to walk home. While heading down the street a few blocks from the hospital, he heard a motorcycle coming in his direction. The biker pulled up on the sidewalk in front of him. He got off the motorcycle but didn't take his helmet off.

Gabe sensed something wasn't right. He started to cross the street when the man called out, "Schaffer, I need to talk to you." Gabe saw the man pull a gun from inside his jacket just as a bus was passing in front of him.

Panicking, Gabe took off as fast as he could, his speed limited by his injured leg. He disappeared down the stairs to a T station. Gabe was breathless as he watched the door to the subway car close without the motorcyclist entering. Perhaps he had escaped for now, but someone was after him, and Gabe didn't know who it was or even what the man looked like.

He needed help. Gabe was in big trouble and didn't know where to turn. Then the thought of someone who might be able to help him popped into his head...someone who knew the streets of Boston better than anyone else. After exiting the subway Gabe called Springhill Penitentiary, and asked to speak to his patient, Aaron Sharpton.

"Aaron, this is Gabe Schaeffer calling. I'm in a huge jam and could really use your assistance."

"Doc, what's up? You sound pretty hassled."

"Well, I was just chased by some guy with a gun, and luckily managed to get away."

"Say, did you get one of your patients really pissed off at you or something?"

"Aaron, this is no joke. The man pulled a gun out and looked like he was about to shoot me, but I was able to get away. I'm afraid he might be successful the next time."

"Doc, you're serious about this, aren't you?"

"Yes, I'm *dead* serious."

"Well, Doc Schaeffer, I wish I could personally handle your problem, but I'm stuck here in Springhill for the next thirty or so years. What I can do is make a phone call to a friend on the outside. His name is Tyrone Jackson. I'll get hold of him, and ask that he keep a close eye on you. TJ has been running things since I was arrested. I can guarantee you he'll give better protection than any police detail."

"That's a pretty tall order, Aaron."

"Don't worry, Doc, I'm not going to let anything bad happen to my shrink. TJ will have your back, count on it. Just go about your daily activities as usual. My man will be watching to make sure you're OK."

The following day as Gabe left Boston General, he noticed a black man sitting on the building stairs talking on his cell phone. As Gabe passed by and looked at him, their eyes meet. The man nodded his head, and Gabe knew it must be TJ. He proceeded to walk down the street as TJ followed at a distance to remain inconspicuous.

After walking a mile, Gabe spotted someone approaching wearing a trench coat, which seemed out of place for the weather.

The man was hardly an imposing figure, but he stopped directly in front of Gabe, blocking his path, then reached inside his coat and pulled out a gun.

Assuming it was a robbery, Gabe produced his wallet and said, "Here, you can have all my money."

The man surprised Gabe by saying, "I don't want your fucking money. I want the formula for OX312. What we are going to do is walk back to your research lab and remove the hard drives from all your computers. I'm certain they have the information I'm looking for."

***

The person, who had assailed Gabe, was Dan Evans, who went by his agency alias, Alex. Evans decided he had been a courier for the agency long enough. He wanted to take advantage of the temporary disruption in authority at the top, with his boss Mueller's sudden departure, to do some freelancing. Why not get the formula for OX312 and sell it to the highest bidder? It didn't matter to him if it was the Chinese, Russians, or Iranians who bought the drug formula as long as it made him rich in the process. He would then take an early retirement, leave the agency, and live in luxury on some Caribbean island.

***

"Are you sure you want to do this?" Gabe asked.

"Don't be a smartass with me just because you happen to be a doctor. You could easily be a *dead* doctor if I get pissed off, so let's get going." Evans motioned with his gun for Gabe to turn around and walk.

Gabe led the way, with his assailant holding a gun at his back. As they proceeded in the direction of Boston General, several tough-looking young black men walked toward them. Soon they were joined by an additional cadre, which flanked them from the side and rear. Only feet separated the group who now surrounded Alex and Gabe.

TJ, their leader, spoke. "Hey, motherfucker, I'd let Dr. Schaeffer go right now if you know what's good for you."

"Is that right?" Evans said, snickering as he exposed the weapon he carried. "As you see, I've got a gun, and I'll use it if you don't back off."

The men began chuckling as TJ spoke again. "Say, cracker, you call that little thing you're holding a gun?" Pulling a Mac-10 from under his jacket, TJ held up the machine gun pistol for Evans to see. "Now, this is what I call a gun!"

At the same time, the other members of his gang pulled out their guns, then locked and loaded. The sound of all the weaponry being prepared to fire rattled Evans to the bone. The man who was so brazen a moment before began perspiring and trembling. Barely able to hold the gun in his quivering hand, Evans laid it down on the sidewalk, then slowly stood up with his hands held aloft.

"OK, guys. No harm meant."

"That's much better," TJ said. "I'm glad you understand the situation. Now, if I ever find out you caused any grief for Dr. Schaeffer in the future, you're a dead man, and I don't give second warnings. So get your Caucasian ass the hell out of here."

Evans took off running down the street and around the block. The group of toughs who bailed Gabe out were hooting and hollering, celebrating their victory.

Once inside his car, Gabe's assailant noticed an enlarging wet spot on the front of his slacks. The Vice Lords had scared him so bad, Evans had wet himself.

41

Gabe's study with the prison inmates at Springhill was completed, and the results were unmistakably positive for OX312 in modifying the tendency for violent behavior. It even looked like there were lingering long-term benefits for those who took the drug; when they stopped their medication after the research ended, most maintained a peaceful demeanor.

Life was much quieter for Gabe now that Vanessa was gone. He focused on his work, and in his limited spare time went sailing. Even though Gabe knew the precise location in the brain where the emotions of love and violence arose, he still had a hard time understanding how he had developed such an overwhelming attraction for a woman he barely knew.

Although he hadn't heard anything from Angela since she left to work for Novara in Switzerland, Gabe frequently thought about her. He wished he could see her again and apologize for his foolish behavior. Angela had always been someone he cared for. He hoped she would be able to forgive him someday.

Gabe finished seeing his patients in clinic and dictating charts by six o'clock. From there he walked to the Shamrock for dinner. Inside the pub, a band was playing. The music and alcohol had the patrons' spirits running high. Gabe placed his order and waited. When the food arrived, he ate, with his thoughts the only company.

Then he heard someone behind him ask, "Anything else I can get for you?"

The voice was different from the waitress who had just served him, yet familiar. Suddenly, it dawned on him whom it belonged to. Gabe pivoted around, almost falling out of his chair. Angela stood in front of him.

"Sorry, Gabe, I didn't mean to startle you."

He quickly swallowed the food he still had in his mouth, then said, "What a surprise? Please sit down and join me." Gabe stood up slowly, due to his injured leg, and pulled out a chair for his unexpected guest.

"Are you all right?" she asked with a concerned look on her face. "It looks like you've been hurt."

Gabe was almost too embarrassed to tell her the truth, but he did. "Angela, Vanessa and I went on a trip to Aspen. She shot me on a hike in the mountains."

"What a terrible accident."

"It was no accident. It turns out she worked for a government agency that wanted our OX312, and wanted it so bad they used her as a tool to manipulate me in order to get it. When I refused to cooperate, she shot me."

"Jesus," Angela said, "I never would have thought—"

"Well, neither did I and that nearly cost me my life. All I'm left with now is a limp, and a terribly bruised ego. Thankfully, according to my physical therapist, in another few weeks I should be back to normal."

"Well, I'm glad you're making a speedy recovery," Angela said, reassured by his prognosis. Then she coyly asked, "Where is Ms. Trent?"

"About a week later, some hikers on the mountain came across the decomposing body of a woman. The autopsy suggested attack by a wild animal, most likely a mountain lion."

"That's awful, but in view of everything you just told me, I have to say good riddance to that bitch."

"Sadly, her remains were unclaimed. According to the police, there is no one named Vanessa Trent." Gabe sighed, then continued. "You know, it's odd, but I'm sure she could have killed me if she really wanted to. I was standing less than twenty feet away when she took her shot."

"Well, if I'd had a gun before I left for Switzerland, I might have shot you first," Angela said jokingly.

"OK, I get the message. But now you must tell me, what brings you back to Boston?"

"Well, a lot has happened since I left town. But I have to be honest with you about a few things. Your secretary, Mary Ann, and I have been communicating. She filled me in on a few of the details about what went on in my absence. Not everything you told me just now came as a surprise." Angela took a deep breath and continued. "I think you probably know I liked you a lot, Gabe, maybe even loved you. But I have to set the record straight."

"Set the record straight about what?"

"The night we made love, do you remember?"

"How could I ever forget?"

"Well, Gabe, I had wanted you so badly, and for so long that I put some OX312 in your wine during dinner." She looked down, in shame. "I'm so sorry. I should never have done anything so deceitful. It put you in an uncomfortable position."

"I would hardly say that what we did that night was uncomfortable. It was actually quite wonderful."

"Do you really mean that?"

"Yes, I do!"

Angela's expression suddenly lit up. Then Gabe continued. "But I need to make a confession to you as well, and this is the right time to do it. It's been weighing on my conscience ever since that same night."

"OK. For God's sake, tell me what you are talking about."

"Well, when you went to visit the bathroom during dinner at the Yankee Clipper, I had brought along a dose of OX312 and planned to slip it into your Diet Coke."

"You did?"

"Yes, but I chickened out at the last minute. I couldn't bring myself to do it, even though I really wanted to. Angela, I've had very strong feelings for you since the day we started working together but kept them pretty much locked inside. I was afraid an emotional relationship would interfere with our work."

"Oh, Gabe!" she exclaimed. Unable to restrain herself any longer, Angela got up from her seat, walked to his side of the table, and kissed him deeply.

He suddenly pulled back and looked into her eyes. "I hope you're not contemplating going back to Switzerland anytime soon."

"Well, now let me tell you my story." She sat back down and began. "After I arrived in Bern, I found Novara provided a tremendous amount of support for my work. They were extremely interested in getting OX312 available for commercial use as soon as possible. The marketing department had even picked out a name, *Aphrodesia*. Unfortunately, Holfield lied to me."

"What do you mean?"

"He planned to sell the drug to anyone who wanted to use it as a 'love potion.' I insisted it be restricted to prescription by licensed psychologists or psychiatrists for use with married couples undergoing therapy. When I saw that Holfield really didn't give a damn about what I felt, I decided to pick up and leave. OX312 has such a powerful effect on the emotion of love, it cannot be used haphazardly."

"You are preaching to the choir," Gabe said, nodding in agreement.

"But something else happened that was even more of a shock. Holfield suddenly disappeared. I never got a straight story as to what transpired, but one day he was gone. Gustav Jung, the Novara CEO, met with me. He told me he understood my desire to return to Boston and apologized for Holfield's outrageous behavior. Jung offered to make amends. He promised to abide by my wishes regarding the restricted use of OX312. He also agreed that Novara would seek approval for an additional indication, use in persons with a tendency to explosive aggression. Gabe you'll be able to have all the OX312 you need for treating your patients, while I use it for couples whose relationships are teetering on the brink of collapse."

"That sounds great."

"Yes. Jung impressed me as an upstanding person, and I trust him at his word. One more thing, He gave me this in compensation for all the hardship Holfield caused." She pulled out a check from her purse and placed it in Gabe's hand. It was made out payable to Angela Chen for $75,000.

"This is incredible!" Gabe exclaimed, looking at Angela in awe.

"Maybe now you could trade in that old boat of yours for a new forty-footer."

"Are you serious?"

"You're darn right, I'm serious. And I'd be happy to be first mate on your new yacht."

Gabe grabbed Angela around the waist, and his embrace lifted her feet off the ground. They kissed long and passionately as the band played in the background. People sitting at the surrounding tables began clapping at the unabashed public display of affection. Soon everyone in the pub joined in giving them a standing ovation. The happy couple briefly turned to the clapping patrons, and waved in acknowledgment, then commenced with another lingering kiss. Angela and Gabe were very much in love, but this time without taking any OX312.

Made in the USA
San Bernardino, CA
30 March 2015